Kiss me.

The stray thought caught her off guard and she jerked away from temptation, stumbling like a klutz over a box. Brandon grabbed her before she fell. The warmth from his hands sent heat coursing through her body. This was so not good.

"Thanks," Arden said breathlessly.

Brandon raised an eyebrow and stared at her as if he knew what she'd been thinking. "Don't you want to know what he said?"

"Who?"

"John." She must have looked as blank as she felt because he spoke the next words very slowly. "The guy who's fixing your car."

"Oh, yeah. Right. What did he say?"

"He towed it in, but he needs the keys. Once we get this stuff inside, I'll drop you off at the garage."

The thought of sitting shoulder to shoulder again in the cab of his truck, his masculine scent swirling around her, tempted her to forget she wasn't interested in getting involved with another man. "You don't have to do that."

"It's not a problem," Brandon replied as he hoisted a box onto his right shoulder.

Then he glanced at the woman before him and wondered, not for the first time, what the heck he was doing.

SWEET BRIAR SWEETHEARTS:
There's something about Sweet Briar...

Dear Reader,

Welcome back to Sweet Briar, North Carolina, where love is in the air once more.

Arden Wexford appears to have it all. She's beautiful and wealthy with a loving, if overprotective, family. But appearances only tell half the story. In her short life, people have pretended to be her friends while actually wanting to get their hands on her money. That includes her skunk of an ex-boyfriend. She yearns for real friends who care about her, not about gaining access to her bank account.

Brandon Danielson has one love in his life—his restaurant. Why? It doesn't lie or pretend to be something that it isn't. Too bad the same can't be said of women like his former fiancée.

Arden and Brandon have each vowed never to fall in love again. I'm betting that they will. The heart, while not the smartest organ in the body, is definitely the most determined. Not to mention that they each find something about the other too appealing to resist.

The Waitress's Secret, the second book in my Sweet Briar Sweethearts series, was a joy to write.

I had so much fun watching two people fight not only falling in love, but against their true natures. Brandon has decided not to be a hero again, but he's fighting a losing battle. He is heroic, and once he accepts that fact, he's all the happier for it. Though Arden may think she is wary and bitter, she can't stay that way for long, because she is really a happy, bubbly person.

I hope you get as much pleasure from reading this book as I got from writing it. I love hearing from my readers, so as always, I invite you to visit my website, kathydouglassbooks.com, and drop me a line. While there, you can sign up for my newsletter. I'm also on Facebook.

Happy reading!

Kathy

The Waitress's Secret

Kathy Douglass

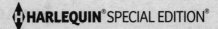

Recycling programs
for this product may
not exist in your area.

ISBN-13: 978-0-373-62373-0

The Waitress's Secret

Copyright © 2017 by Kathleen Gregory

All rights reserved. Except for use in any review, the reproduction or utilization of this work in whole or in part in any form by any electronic, mechanical or other means, now known or hereinafter invented, including xerography, photocopying and recording, or in any information storage or retrieval system, is forbidden without the written permission of the publisher, Harlequin Enterprises Limited, 225 Duncan Mill Road, Don Mills, Ontario M3B 3K9, Canada.

This is a work of fiction. Names, characters, places and incidents are either the product of the author's imagination or are used fictitiously, and any resemblance to actual persons, living or dead, business establishments, events or locales is entirely coincidental.

This edition published by arrangement with Harlequin Books S.A.

For questions and comments about the quality of this book, please contact us at CustomerService@Harlequin.com.

® and TM are trademarks of Harlequin Enterprises Limited or its corporate affiliates. Trademarks indicated with ® are registered in the United States Patent and Trademark Office, the Canadian Intellectual Property Office and in other countries.

Printed in U.S.A.

Kathy Douglass came by her love of reading naturally—both of her parents were readers. She would finish one book and pick up another. Then she attended law school and traded romances for legal opinions.

After the birth of her two children, her love of reading turned into a love of writing. Kathy now spends her days writing the small-town contemporary novels she enjoys reading.

This book is dedicated with love and appreciation to the following people:

To my best friend, Joya, who has been a true friend since the day we met. Thanks for reminding me that I wanted to be a writer.

To Ehryck, Teri and Sandra, who celebrated with me when I signed my first contract.

To Lauren Canan, the best critique partner on the planet.

To my editor, Charles Griemsman, who helps make my books better than even I could imagine.

To my mother-in-law and father-in-law, who raised my husband to be the most wonderful man in the world.

To my siblings, for a lifetime of love and support. A special mention to Marc, who actually did refer to his daughters' playpen as Attica.

To my parents, who loved and supported me in everything I did.

And last, but certainly not least, to my husband and sons, who fill my life with love and happiness. I love all of you more than you can ever imagine.

Chapter One

Arden Wexford pounded on the steering wheel, then turned the ignition key one more time. Still dead. Funny how that worked. Apparently the nineteenth time wasn't the charm. Sighing heavily, she got out of her car and slammed the door, releasing a bit of frustration. She looked under the hood even though she didn't have the foggiest idea what she was searching for.

Her great big adventure, as she had been sarcastically referring to it since her beloved Beetle had broken down, wasn't turning out the way she'd planned. If things had gone the way she'd intended, she would be closer to her parents' house in Florida by now. Instead, she was stranded in Nowhere, North Carolina. She wished she'd driven the Mercedes sedan her parents had given her when she'd graduated from college two years ago. But her candy-red Bug felt like a big hug from her brothers. Driving it always made her happy. After the disaster with Michael-the-jerk, she needed cheering.

Now, though, she wished she had driven the old-lady car. She'd be that much farther away from Baltimore and men willing to stoop to the lowest depths to turn her money into theirs. She was done with greedy men. She was going to hole up in her parents' winter home and enjoy life away from the vipers.

If she ever got out of North Carolina.

She kicked the tire of the offending vehicle even though it wasn't to blame for her predicament. It was properly inflated and ready to roll. All it needed was the car to start.

Arden considered turning the key for the twentieth time, but decided against it. Twenty wasn't going to be any luckier than nineteen. And if she didn't want to spend the night on the side of the road hoping that 2,019 was the charm, she needed to start walking.

She locked the car, then dug through her purse and grabbed her cell phone. She glanced at the screen one more time, hoping that service bars would magically appear. None did.

She'd passed a road sign a couple of miles back indicating she was six miles from some town she'd never heard of. Small Briar or something like that. It couldn't be more than four or so miles away. She ran that far most mornings at her health club. Of course the walk would be easier if she wasn't wearing her cute-to-look-at-but-not-good-for-much-else high-heeled sandals. They were perfect for the airplane flight she'd originally planned. But then her brother commandeered the family jet at the last minute to fly to Monte Carlo for a meeting at one of the Wexford luxury hotels. He'd invited her to come along to relax while he worked, but she'd declined. Her brothers might not mind having their pictures appear in gossip rags catering to people enamored of the rich and famous, but she did. So, she'd decided to drive.

Traffic on the highway was light, with cars passing only occasionally. None of the drivers so much as slowed down. Weren't people in the South supposed to be friendly? Not that she blamed them. She'd never pick up a stranger. And, truthfully, she wasn't sure she'd take a ride even if one was offered.

The day had started out warm and breezy with a clear blue sky. Her T-shirt and color-coordinated skirt had been perfect then, but in the past twenty or so minutes, the temperature had plunged. The cool wind made her long for a sweater. Dark clouds were gathering and the sky was growing threatening. The smell of rain filled the air. She remembered hearing something about a storm in the weather forecast, but since she hadn't expected to still be in the area, she hadn't paid close attention.

Arden picked up her pace, hoping to get to shelter before the clouds burst and she got drenched. After walking about a mile, she checked her cell phone for service again. Still none. Amazing. Her car, which couldn't make it from Baltimore to Tampa, had somehow managed time travel, propelling her into the Dark Ages.

Well, there was no use crying over it. She'd just have to keep walking. She eased a foot from her sandal and shook out yet another pebble. Rubbing her right foot on top of her left, she wondered if shoes that cost nearly a thousand dollars shouldn't be as comfortable as they were beautiful.

Arden slid her foot back into her sandal and, after promising herself a good foot massage as soon as she reached civilization, continued her trek to town. She'd taken a handful of steps when a late-model silver pickup pulled to a stop several yards ahead of her. The driver's door opened and a giant of a man got out. He closed the door and walked around to the back of the truck.

He had thick dreadlocks that were pulled back into a ponytail that hung to the middle of his back. His shoulders were so wide that she imagined he took up more than his share of an airline seat. His broad shoulders only emphasized his flat stomach and trim hips.

He was truly handsome, with dark chocolate skin, a jaw that could only be described as rugged and black eyes that quickly scanned her from head to toe before returning to meet her gaze. A shiver that had nothing to do with the temperature danced down her spine.

Although he had not done anything remotely intimidating, every warning her parents and older brothers had drilled into her since birth about stranger danger raced through her mind. Weren't rich kids always at risk of being kidnapped and held for ransom? Arden looked around. There wasn't another car in sight. She was alone on a deserted highway with a huge man. And no cell service. She stumbled back, cursing her high-heeled shoes.

As if sensing her trepidation, the man backed up until he bumped into his truck, his hands raised, palms out. "I'm not going to hurt you. I want to help you. I passed your car a couple miles back. That is, if you're driving a red Beetle."

His voice was deep, and she noted that he spoke in a calm manner as if soothing a child. She nodded.

"You've walked a long way. You still have about two miles to go until you reach Sweet Briar." He looked up at the darkening sky. "There's a severe thunderstorm warning in effect. Hop in and I'll drop you off in town."

Although he seemed harmless, her family's lessons were too deeply ingrained to cast off simply because a guy had a smooth disc-jockey voice.

Arden shook her head. "Thanks. That's really nice of you to offer, but I'll walk. A little rain never hurt anybody. Besides, it's not raining yet. Maybe it won't."

On cue, lightning streaked across the sky, followed by a loud clap of thunder. And then it started to rain.

"I really don't mind giving you a lift."

Arden tilted her head as she stared at him. Something was off. Although the words were correct and his posture nonthreatening, he didn't appear at all pleased to offer her the ride. He was grimacing and seemed to be forcing the words out of his mouth as if he really didn't want to say them. He reminded her of a reluctant twelve-year-old whose mother kept poking him in the back, prodding him to ask a girl to dance. That reluctance certainly didn't engender confidence.

"No, thanks. I'll take my chances with the rain." It was becoming more of a steady downfall by the second but, still, wet was better than dead or whatever else he might have in mind.

Brandon stared at the woman, wondering if she'd lost her mind. Her hair was plastered to her head and water streamed down her face. Her T-shirt, a pale gray with some sort of orange-and-pink design, now clung to her breasts and tiny waist. He had a feeling she had not as yet realized that her top was fast becoming transparent, revealing the lacy white bra she wore beneath it. She was getting soaked to the bone and she wanted to walk?

Of course she did. That was the cherry on top of a perfectly terrible day. He'd wasted hours in a bank being shuffled from person to person as he unsuccessfully tried to straighten out a mess with the restaurant's account. Now he was wasting even more time standing in the pouring rain trying to convince a stubborn woman to accept his help.

He was tired and irritated and ready to put this day behind him, but he couldn't in good conscience leave her to hoof it to town. It was out of the question. His parents and grandparents had raised him too well to leave her stranded. He could practically hear his father reminding him that a gentleman never left a woman in distress while his mother stood in the background, nodding and murmuring in agreement.

He rubbed a hand across his neck.

The woman lifted her cute little chin in hardheaded resolve.

"Look, I can't just leave you here. I have a sister, and I hope someone would stop and offer assistance if her car broke down. I also hope she'd have sense enough to take the ride."

"Even with a man she's never seen before in her life?"

Brandon huffed out a breath. She had him there. "My name is Brandon Danielson. I own a restaurant in Sweet Briar."

He reached into the back pocket of his jeans, removed his driver's license from his wallet and held it up for her to see although he doubted she could read it from the distance that separated them. "This is me. You can keep it if it makes you feel better. Hell, you can drive if that's what it takes for you to feel safe."

She nodded but still looked unsure. "Okay," she finally agreed. "Thanks."

"Thank me after we get out of this storm."

Slipping and sliding on the unpaved shoulder, the woman reached the passenger door. She stepped on the running board of the truck, then grabbed at the hanging strap to pull herself up the rest of the way. Suddenly her foot slid out from under her. Instinctively, he reached out to help her, grabbing her around her impossibly small waist.

The feel of her soft body sent a jolt of awareness surging through him. He set her away as quickly as he could and frowned at the reaction of his body. He was a Good Samaritan, not some player picking up women on the side of the road.

"I'm going to help you into the truck." Before she could respond, he lifted her into his arms and settled her into the passenger seat. Even soaking wet, she couldn't have weighed more than a hundred and fifteen or twenty pounds. Closing her door, he lost no time getting to the other side and slipping behind the wheel. As soon as he started the truck and the air began to circulate, he got a whiff of her scent. Man, she smelled good. Like rain and shampoo—which was expected—but also like sunshine and flowers. Like happiness. Where had that come from? He shook his head slightly in the hope the foolishness would rattle out his ears, then glanced at his passenger.

Even with most of her makeup washed off, she was

incredibly beautiful. She had remarkably clear caramel-colored skin and light brown eyes. With high cheek-bones and a perfectly shaped nose and lips, she could have been a model. Of course, he would have appreciated her beauty more if he didn't need to start building an ark. And, like any beautiful work of art, she was best viewed from a distance. He would do well to keep that in mind.

She returned his glance with wide eyes. Her teeth were chattering, whether from nerves or because she was drenched and cold, he didn't know. Maybe a little of both. He flipped on the heater and edged back onto the road. The wipers were on the fastest setting, yet they could barely keep up with the downfall.

"The truck has heated seats. And there's a jacket in the back you can use."

She moved her hand off the door handle and pressed the button he indicated. "I don't need your jacket. I'm fine. Besides, you're just as wet as I am."

"Maybe." He reached behind the seat and grabbed his denim jacket. "But perhaps you should look at your shirt. You might reconsider."

She looked down and squeaked. "I look like a refugee from a wet T-shirt contest."

He couldn't help chuckling as she took the jacket and draped it over her torso. Although her breasts weren't nearly the size of the women's who entered such contests, they were still appealing. Not that he was looking. Much.

"What's your name?"

The question really wasn't that difficult, yet she hesitated as if trying to find the right answer. "It's Arden… Arden W…West."

"So, Arden, what brings you to North Carolina?"

She raised a suspicious eyebrow and leaned closer to her door. "How do you know I'm not from here?"

"No accent. You don't have that Southern way of speaking."

She nodded. "True."

"And I saw your car, remember? Maryland plates."

"Oh." She heaved out a breath. A bit of remorse fell over her fine features and the stiffness left her spine.

"So, what brings you to our neck of the woods?"

"My car broke down here." Arden had an impish smile on her face, which hit him in the center of his chest with unexpected force, momentarily making breathing hard.

"Sweet Briar is a small town. There's a magnetic field that captures new people and won't let them leave. Sort of like the Hotel California."

"Where you can check out but never leave?"

Brandon nodded, pleased that she understood his reference to the classic Eagles song.

"Are you from here?"

"No."

When he didn't say anything more, she looked at him, her eyebrows raised in question.

"Chicago. I moved here three years ago." A man who preferred to keep things on the surface, he didn't normally volunteer information about himself. But being open seemed to put her at ease. So, as long as they kept to generalities, it was all good.

She tilted her head and looked him over, a mischievous expression on her face. "Did the magnet catch you or did you stay by choice?"

"Choice." He hadn't been able to leave Chicago and

that lying Sylvia fast enough. When a friend mentioned his cousins loved living in Sweet Briar, Brandon had been on the first plane to North Carolina.

Arden nodded, then turned to look out the window. Lightning flashed, followed by loud, booming thunder. The rain was coming down too fast for the drainage system to keep up. At the rate water was beginning to flood the road, he wouldn't be surprised if several streets in town were already closed.

After several frustrating minutes of inching down the highway and ten minutes spent sitting under an overpass when the downpour made driving too hazardous, they finally saw the sign welcoming them to Sweet Briar, population 1,976. He heard his passenger's sigh of relief and wondered if maybe she was more nervous than she let on.

"Is there a hotel where you can drop me? Or, better yet, a garage where I can arrange a tow?"

"No hotel. We only have a couple of bed-and-breakfasts." He wiped the condensation off the windshield and leaned forward for a better look. Just as he thought. There was close to three inches of water on the roads and the level was rising. "We have a garage, but I'm sure John has closed up for the night."

She checked her watch, then glanced over at him, disbelief on her lovely face. "It's only five o'clock."

"He generally closes around four thirty or five. You know, small town."

"I guess." She agreed but still looked doubtful. "Is there another mechanic in town?"

"Nope. Just John. And, to be honest, the way the streets are flooding, he probably wouldn't tow you now anyway."

Arden considered a minute. "Okay. Then I guess you can just drop me at the B and B."

"No problem. The Sunrise B and B is just a couple of blocks away. Call John in the morning. Let him know you're in a hurry and he'll have you back on the road in no time."

"Thanks."

"Kristina will be able to give you John's number. She owns the B and B, by the way."

"Speaking of calling." Arden pulled out her phone and checked it. Grinning, she held it up to him. "Bars. I have bars. I'm out of the seventies."

Brandon blinked. "What?"

She laughed. "I couldn't get service where the car died."

He nodded his understanding. "Ah. Gotcha. Cell service is spotty in this area. It takes some getting used to. But you shouldn't have trouble in town."

"That's good to know."

He pulled in front of an old Victorian mansion that Kristina Harrison had converted into a thriving business.

Arden peered out the window. At that moment, lightning streaked across the sky and thunder rolled. "You called this the *Sunrise* B and B?"

"Yeah."

"It looks more like a haunted house." She glanced at the building and then back at him. "You sure Herman and Lily don't live here?"

He barked out a surprised laugh. So she liked the old sixties television show *The Munsters*. So did he. "I'm positive. Although the name of the street is Mockingbird Lane."

"Are you kidding me? The Munsters lived at 1313 Mockingbird Lane."

"Yeah. I'm kidding. This is Rose Street."

She shook her small fist at him. "That's so not funny."

Brandon resisted the urge to laugh but couldn't suppress a smile. "Yeah, it was."

She grinned with him. "Okay, it was."

"I know this place looks spooky in this storm, but it's actually a well-kept building. And the inside is great. You'll be comfortable."

"Have you ever stayed here?"

"Well, no. I have a house in town. But trust me. Kristina Harrison has great taste. And she's a nice person. You'll be fine."

"Okay."

"Stay here. I'll help you." He was halfway around the front of the truck when the passenger door opened and Arden hopped out. A splash was followed by a squeal.

"I know. I know. Don't say it." She laughed as she stepped onto the curb. "I just thought I could get out and save you the trouble."

He shook his head. How much trouble could it be to help her out of his truck and carry her across a few puddles? Apparently, she'd rather do that crazy hop-tiptoe step through several inches of cold water than wait for his assistance. He understood the need to be independent since he liked to do things for himself as well, so he resisted the urge to sweep her into his arms and carry her to the stairs, even though it meant getting drenched again. He did stay close by, ready to catch her if she stumbled.

She finally slip-slid her way to the stairs and grabbed

a railing. Letting out a breath, he climbed the steps beside her, eager to reach the porch and get them both out of the driving rain. He rang the doorbell and in less than a minute the glass door swung open.

"Goodness. Get in here before you catch pneumonia," Kristina said, motioning for them to enter.

"Thanks." Brandon stepped aside to let Arden go before him.

Arden didn't need to be told twice. She stepped inside the door held open by a pretty woman who looked to be in her midtwenties. Brandon closed the door behind them and made the introductions.

"I'll grab some towels so you can dry off," Kristina said. Arden hated the idea of tracking water across the gleaming marble floors, but when the woman gave her a gentle nudge, she moved toward the sitting room. Two comfy-looking sofas flanked a fireplace that Arden wished was lit. Kristina bustled out of the room.

"Brandon, what brings you and your friend out on such a horrible night?" she said as she hurried back, carrying two fluffy towels. She handed one to Arden, who blotted her face, then began drying her arms.

Brandon took the other towel and smiled at Kristina. For a split second illogical possessiveness and jealousy battled for dominance inside Arden, which didn't make sense. Why should she care who Brandon smiled at? She'd only just met the man. Besides, men were snakes. Just because she hadn't heard him rattle didn't mean he didn't bite. Arden definitely wasn't interested in being bitten again.

As they dried themselves off, Brandon explained about Arden's car breaking down on the highway.

"Oh, you poor thing. How awful," Kristina said, shaking her head.

Brandon rubbed the towel over his face, his enormous chest muscles flexing. A jolt of awareness shot through her, and Arden suddenly went from chilled to overheated. She rubbed the towel over her hair, reminding herself that a beautiful body didn't necessarily translate to a good heart. Though, to be fair, he had been more than kind so far. And he didn't even know she was rich.

"I gave her a lift and brought her here. She needs a place to stay the night."

"Oh, no. I'm booked. Carmen and Trent's wedding is this weekend. People started arriving this afternoon."

"So early? It's only Monday."

"Apparently, some of the guests are turning this trip into a vacation. Sweet Briar has become a popular destination in the past couple years. In fact, I'm filled for most of the summer." Kristina turned to Arden to include her in the conversation. "Trent is our chief of police and a great guy. His first wife was killed in a car accident a few years back. How long ago was it, Brandon?"

He shrugged his massive shoulders. "It was before my time."

Kristina turned back to Arden. "Anyway, Carmen was born here but moved to New York years ago. She came back for her mother's funeral, God rest her soul. Anyhow, they fell in love and are getting married. Don't you just love a happy ending?"

Kristina sighed. Arden sneezed.

"Bless you. I'm so sorry I don't have a place for you to stay. I would suggest the Come On Inn, even though

Reginald Thomas annoys me enough to make me swear, but they're booked, too. Of course we were filled days before they were. They only got our overflow."

Arden nodded and rubbed the towel over her legs. She really needed to get out of these wet clothes.

"So, what are you going to do?" Kristina asked. It was clear to Arden that the other woman was sincerely concerned, which surprised her, given that they were complete strangers.

"The only thing we can do. I'm taking her home with me."

Chapter Two

"You're taking me home with you?" Arden asked the minute they were alone in his truck. "There has to be somewhere else I can stay the night."

Brandon glanced over at Arden. She was watching him almost as closely as she had when he'd picked her up on the highway. He could understand her unease although she had nothing to be afraid of. "You heard Kristina. Both bed-and-breakfasts are filled. There's not another place in town. There are a couple of chain hotels twenty or so miles down the highway, but I'm not sure all the roads are passable. And, even if we make it, there's no guarantee they'll have rooms available."

She nodded, but she didn't appear pleased by his answer. Still, she couldn't argue the facts. The rain showed no sign of letting up anytime soon. Truth be told, he wished there was somewhere else she could spend the night. He'd rather be done with the whole thing, too, but he had picked her up and now bore some responsibility for her welfare. He couldn't just dump her on the side of the road in the middle of a storm and bid her adieu. He'd arrange for her to get her car towed to town first thing in the morning so she could go on her merry way. Surely that would be enough chivalry to satisfy even his parents.

He started the truck and drove down the street, passing the town's lone gas station. The lights over the pumps were dim, casting odd shadows on the street. Not a soul was around. "You'll be perfectly safe. My sister, Joni, lives with me."

"And she'll be there?"

He nodded and stopped at the corner. He grabbed his cell phone, punched in his home number and put the phone on speaker. Joni answered on the third ring.

"Hey, Brandon."

"Joni, I'll be home in a couple of minutes. I'm bringing someone with me."

Joni laughed. "I know. I just got off the phone with Kristina."

"That woman is in the wrong business. She should be a reporter."

Joni laughed again. "Can your friend hear me?"

"Yeah."

Brandon looked at Arden, who smiled tentatively.

"Don't worry. My brother is perfectly harmless. And I know you're soaked to the skin. I have dry clothes ready for you to change into."

"Thanks. I really appreciate it."

"Not a problem."

Brandon ended the call and looked at Arden. "Better?"

She smiled and for a second the sun seemed to break through the clouds. He felt a stirring where his heart used to be and immediately quashed it.

"Much better. Thanks for calling her."

"Sure. I can't have you worried about your safety like some woman in a horror story."

Arden glanced at the dark street. The wind was blowing the trees every which way, casting shadows that shifted so much they looked like arms reaching out to grab something. "It does look kind of creepy out here. Like some chainsaw-wielding maniac could jump from a dark corner and attack us. Well, me anyway. You're kind of big for someone to mess with."

Brandon continued driving. "Don't worry. There's no one hiding in the shadows or anywhere else. And if someone did try to hurt you, I'd protect you."

The grateful look she sent him made his chest grow tight and warmed the cold bitterness in his soul. He rubbed his hand across the raised scar near his heart as a reminder to keep his emotional distance. The last time he'd gotten close to a woman he'd ended up in intensive care. It was okay to be friendly—Arden needed that to be at ease. But genial chatter was one thing; an emotional connection was something entirely different.

"My brothers always said I have a vivid imagination. Which is why I never watch scary movies."

"Never?"

"Not ever. Afterward, I'd be so busy checking under my bed and jumping at every bump in the night that I'd never get any sleep."

He nodded. "That's our house right there. Third one on the left."

Arden leaned back in her seat and sighed. "It looks normal from here."

"We keep the dragon in the basement."

"That's good to know." She leaned forward and peered out the window at the rising water. "What I really want to know is where you keep the rowboat."

"Not interested in wading through the water again?"

"No." She looked down at her ruined sandals. "Once was enough for me. I think I can cross that off my bucket list."

"Walking through rainwater up to your ankles was on your bucket list?"

She lifted the corner of her mouth in a mischievous grin. "I want to have a wide range of experiences."

"I'm glad we could oblige," he said, pulling into the driveway.

Less than a minute later they were running through the large backyard and racing up a flight of stairs. A woman Arden assumed was Brandon's sister opened the door and stepped back to let them inside. She had friendly eyes and introduced herself with a bright smile.

"It's really coming down out there," Joni said, closing the door against the wind. Arden slipped off her damp and muddy sandals and placed them beside the door so she wouldn't track mud through the house. Joni led the way through the utility room and into the kitchen. The room was huge, with restaurant-quality appliances. There were miles of glistening marble countertops. A solid wood farmhouse table sat near an unlit stone fireplace. Wonderful aromas floated in the air and Arden's stomach growled.

"Sorry." Cheeks burning, Arden placed a hand over her stomach, trying to muffle the sound.

Joni waved away Arden's apology. "Don't be. You're not only soaked to the bone, you're also hungry. If I were you I'd be grabbing food from the pots with my bare hands."

Arden laughed, her embarrassment dissipating. She liked Joni.

"I've got some dry clothes for you that will fit better than my brother's jacket. Come on, you can take a quick shower and get warm. You'll feel a lot better. It'll be a few minutes before dinner's ready."

Warm water and dry clothes sounded wonderful. "Are you sure you don't mind? I don't want to put you out."

"Nonsense. It's no bother."

"Thanks."

"The stairs are this way."

Joni put her arm around Arden in a sisterly way and led her farther into the house. Although Arden had run as fast as she dared through the slippery yard, she'd still gotten drenched again. She hated dripping onto the beautiful hardwood floor, but she couldn't strip in the kitchen.

Joni didn't seem to mind about the mess, and seconds later they were climbing a flight of stairs. Brandon followed them in silence.

"You can use this room," Joni said, opening a door to a bedroom and stepping through to the en suite. "Brandon had some renovations done to the house when we moved here. He turned a couple of tiny rooms into bathrooms. I didn't agree with his decision at first, but I totally love it now."

As she talked, Joni bustled about the room, pulling plush towels out of a linen closet, then stacking them on the marble counter. She grabbed bottles of shampoo and conditioner and several different types of body wash from a cabinet beside the sink. "I'll be right back."

Arden nodded, grateful when the other woman returned with a stack of dry clothes.

After Joni left, Arden took one look in the mirror and groaned. Her makeup was completely washed off, but her face was far from clean. Somehow mud had gotten spattered on her cheeks, with one long smear down the side of her face. Her wet hair was wind whipped and going in every direction. She ran her hand through it and discovered a leaf-covered twig had gotten tangled in her mane, completing the puppy-playing-in-a-mud-puddle look. She stripped and stepped into the shower.

A moan of pure pleasure escaped her lips as the hot water began to warm her, slowing the chatter of her teeth. No shower had ever felt this good. If it wasn't for the fact that her hosts were waiting for her, she'd spend the next hour letting the warm water pound every ache out of her body. As a guest, an unexpected one at that, it would be rude to linger.

She hurriedly poured shampoo into her hands and quickly lathered her hair. Joni used the same brand she did and the familiar scent soothed the last of Arden's nerves. Her remaining tension disappeared down the drain with the bubbles.

She gathered her wet clothes and placed them on the counter. She would ask Joni where she could launder them later. Joni had left an assortment of clothes and she sorted through them before selecting a long-sleeved cotton top and denim pants. The jeans were a little long, so she rolled them up before pulling on socks and heading downstairs.

When she'd entered the house, she'd been too cold and uncomfortable to give more than a cursory glance at her surroundings. Now, though, she looked carefully. The house was a wonderful blend of old charm and modern convenience. The rooms had wide baseboards and crown molding around the high ceilings. Painted white, they were a nice accent to the darker-colored walls.

The furniture in the living room, while stylish, had clearly been chosen for comfort. With randomly placed pillows and a throw tossed over a leather ottoman, this room was used for living and not just for show.

Arden heard voices coming from the back of the house and followed them to the kitchen. The aromas wafting through the air reminded her that it had been hours since she'd eaten lunch. If scarfing down a hot dog and bag of chips in her car qualified as eating lunch.

"Come sit down. Dinner is just about ready." Joni pointed to a seat at the table. A small vase of wildflowers was in the center. The curtains were closed so Arden couldn't see the storm. She could hear it, though. The rain pounded on the windows like it was trying to get in, and the wind howled like an injured animal. This was definitely not a night to be outside. And if it wasn't for Brandon, she'd be out in this wicked weather.

Arden glanced at Brandon. He'd changed into a gray polo shirt that pulled tight across his barrel chest and loose-fitting jeans that couldn't disguise his muscular thighs. The man put all the statues she'd studied in her art-history class to shame.

She shook her head. What was wrong with her? She'd seen plenty of handsome men in her life, yet she didn't gawk at them like some teenager with no home training. "I can't thank you enough for your hospitality and the clothes, Joni. I'll return them as soon as possible."

Joni smiled. "Don't worry about it. I have way more clothes than I need." She then fixed her brother with a mock glare. "Don't say a word."

"I didn't open my mouth."

"Good."

"But if I had said anything, it would be that you have more clothes than any three people need." Joni tossed a linen napkin at him. He caught it with ease and dropped it onto the counter. Then he pulled open the oven door for a quick look and nodded with apparent satisfaction.

Arden watched them banter back and forth with a smile on her face. It was clear to her they not only loved each other, they genuinely liked each other. They were friends.

She sighed wistfully. She wished she could say the same of her relationship with her brothers. She knew they loved her. They'd do anything for her. But Blake and Jax were stuck in protective-big-brother mode. To them, she was still the child who got into jams and waited for them to bail her out, which they'd done without fail. She'd grown up, but they hadn't noticed. Because they didn't view her as an adult, their relationship hadn't evolved to the point of friendship.

And the near disaster with Michael-the-sneak wouldn't help them see her as an equal. Which was why she had told them only that she'd ended the relationship, keeping the disgusting details to herself.

Brandon stirred, then began ladling soup out of a

pot into large bowls while Joni placed warm bread on the table.

"Is there anything I can do to help?" Arden asked, shoving aside the depressing thoughts.

"Not a thing," Joni said, taking the bowls from her brother and setting one before Arden. "Just relax."

Brandon joined them. As he scooted his chair closer to the table, the scent of soap teased her nostrils and her heart began to beat double time. He looked at her expectantly, waiting for her to sample her food before he ate.

Arden picked up a spoon and sipped her soup. Incredible flavors exploded in her mouth. She'd eaten at some of the best restaurants in the world, but nothing compared to this Italian sausage soup. Before she could stop it, a moan of unadulterated pleasure slipped from between her lips.

Brandon stared at her, his dark eyes unreadable. For a moment their gazes locked and time stood still. Her breath caught in her throat. Trapped like a fly in a web, Arden couldn't look away to save her life.

"My, my," Joni said with a laugh, looking from Brandon to Arden.

Joni's voice broke the spell, freeing Arden from Brandon's hypnotic gaze.

"Sorry." She looked down at the bowl to hide her embarrassment. *What is wrong with me?* She looked at Joni. "This soup is the best thing I've ever tasted in my life. You're a great cook."

Joni shook her head. "Not me. I can't toast bread without burning it. Brandon is the chef."

Arden risked a glance at him, warning herself not to get caught in those dark, amazing eyes again. "You made this? Wow. It's wonderful."

"Thanks." His voice sounded strained and low. He'd been charming in the car, but now he seemed more reserved with her. It was as if he regretted their earlier camaraderie.

"Brandon is chef and owner of the most popular restaurant in the state. Heaven on Earth."

"The name fits," Arden added, wishing her bowl was larger. She'd just hit bottom when Brandon removed her empty dish. A couple moments later he returned with three plates.

"Be careful," Brandon said, setting the dishes on the table. "It's hot."

"This looks wonderful. What is it?"

"Oven-roasted sea bass with oranges, tomatoes and olives."

Arden stared at him in amazement. "You made all of this while I was in the shower?"

"No. I prepared it earlier today. Joni put it in the oven when we got home."

She took a bite and this time managed to stifle the sound of pleasure that threatened to escape. The perfect combination of flavors was unlike anything she had ever experienced, even during the summer after high school she'd spent in France and Italy.

Joni sipped her drink, then looked at Arden. "Where were you headed when your car broke down?"

"Don't be so nosy," Brandon said, shaking his head.

Joni waved away his comment like she would a pesky gnat, then looked at Arden expectantly. Ordinarily Arden would be annoyed by such a personal question from a complete stranger. But Joni didn't feel like a stranger, she felt like a friend. "I'm on my way to Florida."

"For vacation? A new job?"

Arden shook her head. "Neither. I just need to get away for a while."

"From what?" Brandon asked, apparently forgetting the no-prying rule.

"I thought we weren't going to be nosy," Joni pointed out.

Brandon glared playfully at his sister, then smiled at Arden. "Sorry. Forget I said anything."

"No, it's okay. A relationship I was in ended badly. I just needed some space to get my head together. I'm a middle school science teacher, so I'm off for the summer. Since there was nothing holding me in town, I decided to get out while the getting was good."

"So…what are your plans when you get to Florida?" Joni asked.

Brandon shook his head at his sister but did appear interested in Arden's answer.

"I don't really have plans," Arden confessed. Suddenly, sitting alone in her parents' home hiding from the world and licking her wounds lost its appeal. It actually sounded pretty pathetic. Was she so fragile that she needed weeks in seclusion because her boyfriend had turned out to be a jerk? Heck, no. Double heck, no. She was stronger than that.

"And now you're stuck in Sweet Briar." Brandon finished his meal and pushed his plate into the center of the table. She did the same. "John's good. He'll have you back on the road in no time."

He stood and began clearing the table. Before she or Joni could move, he'd rinsed the plates and bowls and loaded them into the dishwasher. When that task was complete, he excused himself and left the kitchen.

Arden watched him leave, noting once again what a

fine specimen of a man he was. He was the definition of masculinity. She might not be in the market for a man, but she wasn't opposed to window-shopping. Realizing she was gawking at Brandon in front of his sister, she pulled her gaze away and reached for her coffee cup. She stifled her attraction before it could turn into interest or something more. She might not know much, but she knew better than to let her emotions get the upper hand on her common sense. No way. She wasn't going to open herself up even for a minute and end up getting hurt again.

Thankfully, she wasn't going to be around long enough to put that theory to the test. As soon as her car was fixed she was out of Sweet Briar.

Chapter Three

Arden woke to the sound of birds chirping and a dog barking in the distance. Stretching languidly, she smiled and opened her eyes. Momentarily startled by the unfamiliar surroundings, she jerked upright to a sitting position. A heartbeat later she remembered everything: her car breaking down, Brandon rescuing her and bringing her to his home.

Slipping from the bed, Arden crossed the room to the en suite. Not a morning person by nature, she felt unusually refreshed. She credited her vigor to the early hour she'd gone to bed and the fact that she'd slept like the proverbial baby.

She brushed her teeth, washed up and applied some lip gloss. After dressing in the clothes she'd washed last night, she tidied the bathroom and made her bed. When she stepped into the hallway she heard voices, so she knew Brandon and Joni were awake. Following the sound, Arden arrived at the kitchen.

"Good morning," Joni said from her seat at the table. "Help yourself to some coffee."

"Thanks." Arden grabbed a mug from beside the coffeemaker, filled it, and added sugar and amaretto cream.

"Brandon and I were just talking about you."

"Were you?"

"Yes," Brandon replied.

Until he spoke, Arden had avoided looking at him. Now, though, she forced her gaze to where he leaned near the window. She'd thought he was to-die-for gorgeous yesterday, but it was nothing compared to the way he looked this morning. His jaw was scraped clean of all stubble and appeared baby-bottom smooth. She curled her hand into a fist to resist the urge to caress his face and find out. His dreadlocks were hanging loose around his shoulders. Dressed in a simple white T-shirt, his denim-clad legs crossed at the ankle, he looked perfectly relaxed.

Although her heart thumped wildly in her chest at the sight of him, she managed to speak normally. "Do I want to know what you were saying, or should I go back upstairs?"

He smiled. "We were discussing your situation."

His smile momentarily stopped her brain from functioning. "What situation?"

"Your car."

"Right." She took a swallow of her coffee, hoping a jolt of caffeine would help her follow a simple conversation.

"I talked to John. He'll tow it to his garage this morning and get to work on it as soon as he can. I didn't know your cell phone number, so I told him to call me when he knows what the problem is and has an estimate. Does that work for you?"

She nodded. He'd handled everything with one phone call, saving her the hassle and the stress. She knew she should be grateful, and she was. If only he didn't remind her of her brothers rushing in to save the day. "That works great. Thanks."

"Sure." He glanced at his watch, then pushed away from the wall. "I need to get to the restaurant. I'll catch up with you two later."

Arden managed to keep her eyes from following him as he left.

"How about breakfast?" Joni asked. From the twinkle in her eyes, she hadn't missed Arden's struggle to not watch Brandon leave.

"Breakfast sounds great. But you told me you're not much of a cook and, to be honest, neither am I. The best cook just left the house."

Joni laughed. "I didn't mean here. Brandon would lose his mind if I touched his precious stove without his written permission and step-by-step instructions. There's a great diner in town where everyone goes for breakfast. Even Brandon, and he doesn't make a practice of eating other people's cooking."

"Okay. I'm in."

Ten minutes later Arden and Joni entered Mabel's Diner. The place looked exactly like Arden imagined a small-town diner should. Red vinyl booths lined the walls. Square tables with chrome chairs with red vinyl cushions filled the middle of the room. Framed pictures of movie stars hung on the walls at odd intervals. An old-fashioned jukebox played an ancient doo-wop song. It was positively charming.

Several people called hello to Joni, who returned their greetings. Every booth was filled, so Joni led the way to one of the tables. Arden grabbed a laminated menu from between an old-fashioned sugar bowl and the salt-and-pepper shakers. There was so much to choose from. Omelets, waffles, pancakes, bacon, sausage, even pork chops and fish.

After looking over the selections, she glanced up at Joni, whose menu remained untouched. "You already know what you want?" Arden didn't know how she was going to decide what to eat. She loved food and considered eating her hobby. Fortunately, she had a high metabolism or she'd be the size of a sumo wrestler.

Joni nodded. "The special on Tuesday is excellent. Grits, breakfast potatoes, two sausage links, two strips of bacon, two pancakes and two eggs cooked any way you want as long as you want them fried."

"All for two dollars?" Arden quipped.

Joni didn't laugh or even smile. Instead, she placed her hand on Arden's and gave a squeeze. "Don't worry about the cost. Breakfast is on me."

Arden had opened her mouth to correct Joni's misconception about her finances when the waitress stepped up to their table, pad in hand and ready to take their orders.

"Hi, I'm Lynn and I'll be your server. Are you ready?"

Joni nodded at the perky teenager. "I know what I want. What about you, Arden?"

"I think I'll try the special."

"Good choice," Joni said. "Two specials."

"Okay." The waitress scribbled down their orders and promised to return right away with their orange juice.

"You don't have to buy me breakfast. I have money."

"And a broken-down car. My mother is a teacher and I know they don't make much money. Especially new ones."

"I know how this must look, but—"

"No buts. Just accept breakfast with the same good grace you accepted our hospitality last night. Simply smile and say thanks."

Having someone offer to pay for anything was a new experience for Arden. Usually it was the other way around. People sat on their hands waiting for Arden to whip out her wallet and pay for their meals. And if someone did treat her, it was only because they wanted something in return. Joni didn't know she was a Wexford, so she obviously didn't have an ulterior motive. Joni was being nice because she was a nice person.

Still, she didn't feel right leaving Joni with the wrong impression. It felt like lying by omission. And she hated liars. But Joni was adamant about buying breakfast and Arden didn't want to insult her by refusing her offer. She'd let Joni buy her breakfast now and she'd treat Joni later.

Arden smiled. "Thanks. I really appreciate it."

"You're welcome," Joni replied.

Their waitress returned with their food, setting the plates before them. Arden picked up her fork, breathing in the delicious aromas. As they ate, Joni told Arden about life in Sweet Briar. She mentioned little tidbits about the different residents, but none of it was mean-spirited or gossipy. From what Arden heard and saw, Sweet Briar was almost too good to be believed.

When they finished eating, Joni took several bills from her wallet and dropped them on the table.

"I should at least leave the tip," Arden offered, rummaging through her purse.

"Not a chance. But if you want, you can help out at the youth center. I need to get some things together before the kids arrive."

"Sure. Whatever you need."

"Great."

After a short drive Joni pulled into a paved parking lot in front of a three-story building. Arden had come to think of Sweet Briar as a quaint town, so the dynamic mural with graffiti art wrapping around the outside of the building came as a pleasant surprise.

Joni looked with pride at the building. "The youth center was built by the city, but the tax dollars we receive only go so far. Donations and grants keep us afloat. At least most of the time. We're popular with the kids, though, and we're filling a need. That's what matters."

Joni popped open the trunk and grabbed a couple of boxes. Arden did the same and followed her inside. The trunk was loaded with bags and boxes so she knew several trips would be necessary. Joni turned off the alarm and flipped on the lights. "Just drop everything on the front counter for now."

Arden set down her load and looked around. The most fabulous mural drew her attention and she crossed the room to get a better look.

"What do you think?" Joni asked, walking up behind her.

"It's great. Very dynamic." And that was putting it mildly. It was one of the best pieces of art she'd ever seen. Not that she was an expert by any stretch of the imagination. But she had been dragged to art galleries more times than she cared to remember and had been exposed to top-tier art. This was definitely of that quality. It was not something she expected to see in a small-town youth center.

"Isn't it? The artist is Carmen Taylor. She grew up here and moved to New York some years ago, where she did quite well. From what I understand, she's very famous in the art world. She donated this mural and designed the one outside. Volunteers painted that one, but she did this one herself. She's getting married Saturday."

"To the chief of police. Trent somebody."

Joni arched her eyebrows. "My, my. You haven't been in town twenty-four hours and already you're in the know."

"Not really. Kristina Harrison mentioned the wedding yesterday. The bed-and-breakfast is full of wedding guests, which is why I couldn't stay there."

"Brandon is catering the rehearsal dinner and the reception. It's quite the coup. A few bigwigs from New York are coming. This could really help Brandon out."

"I thought his restaurant was doing well."

"It is. But he always says that if you aren't growing and moving up, you're stagnating and on your way down."

Arden nodded. She'd heard her father and brothers make similar statements over the years. Even though Wexford Industries was a huge corporation, the principle still applied.

"Come on, let's grab the rest."

When they stepped outside, Arden saw Brandon reaching into Joni's trunk, two boxes near his feet while he hefted out another. His shirt was taut across the muscles of his back as they flexed with his movement. Arden's mouth watered at the sight, but she managed to keep from drooling.

"What are you doing here?" Joni asked, leaning against the bumper.

"John called. I forgot to get Arden's number and, as usual, your phone is turned off."

"Oops." Joni didn't sound even the tiniest bit sorry. She shrugged, picked up a couple of bags and carried them inside.

Arden grabbed a box, eager to get away from the gorgeous man before she did something ridiculous like flirt or bat her eyelashes. The weight inside shifted and the box began to slip. Brandon reached out to help her steady the load. His hand brushed against her arm and her knees actually went weak. Her eyes flew to his and time seemed to stop. She found herself swaying closer to him.

Kiss me. The stray thought caught her off guard and she jerked away from temptation, stumbling like a klutz over a box beside him. He grabbed her before she fell. The warmth from his hands sent heat coursing through her body. This was so not good.

"Thanks," Arden said breathlessly, and took a step toward the youth center, hoping to get away and gather herself.

Brandon raised an eyebrow and stared at her as if he knew what she'd been thinking. "Don't you want to know what he said?"

"Who?"

"John." She must have looked as blank as she felt because he spoke the next words very slowly. "The guy who's fixing your car."

"Oh, yeah. Right. What did he say?"

"He towed it in, but he needs the keys. Once we get this stuff inside, I'll drop you off at the garage."

The thought of their sitting shoulder to shoulder again in the cab of Brandon's truck, his masculine scent swirling around her, tempted her to forget she was not interested in getting involved with another man. "You don't have to do that. I've caused you enough trouble as it is."

"It's not a problem," Brandon replied as he hoisted a box onto his right shoulder and grabbed another under his left arm. "John's place is on the way to my restaurant."

Brandon glanced at the woman beside him and wondered, not for the first time, what the heck he was doing. Although he'd previously had no problem keeping women at arm's distance, he was being drawn into Arden's orbit. Worse, he was doing nothing to resist her pull. He knew Joni would have dropped Arden off at John's garage, but instead he heard himself offering her a ride. What was it about her that had his mouth running miles ahead of his brain and leading his body in the totally wrong direction?

Sure, she was pretty and liked some of the same things he did. Before Sylvia's treachery, that would have been a good thing and he would have pursued her. Now… If he knew what was good for him he would stay away from her before she drew him in and made him feel things he didn't want to feel ever again.

The morning was warm with the promise of becoming a scorcher as the day wore on. The sun was shining in the cloudless sky so he pulled down the visor. Still, the sun was no match for the brilliance of Arden's smile.

It was almost hot enough to melt the ice encasing his heart. Almost. Lucky for him she was leaving soon or he might be in danger of letting her get too close.

She peered out the window. "Sweet Briar has got to be the cutest place I've ever seen."

He bit back a sigh of relief. Talking about impersonal things was safe and easy. Figuring out his attraction to her and how to get control of it was not. "Our town is making a better impression on you today than last night?"

"Oh, yeah. I can't believe the difference a little sunlight makes. It looks like a picture postcard, advertising the perfect little town. The shops are so pretty with their striped awnings and old-fashioned signs. Best of all there's not a chain restaurant in sight to ruin the effect. There's not a stray branch or leaf in sight, either. If I hadn't lived through it, I wouldn't believe a storm blew through here only hours ago. It's like elves or fairies cleaned up everything overnight."

"Fairies and elves?"

"Okay. Shop owners." Understanding lit her eyes. "That's what you were doing this morning. Clearing the street and walkways around your restaurant."

"Guilty as charged."

He drove past Wilson's Hardware and waved at Hank, grandson of the founder. Two doors down, Carlo and Mario Marconi were setting red-and-white-checkered tablecloths, vinyl place mats and napkin-wrapped silverware on the tables in front of their family-owned pizza parlor.

"Ooh."

"What?"

"Do you see that?" Arden's reverent whisper made

her sound like a kid looking at a pile of presents under the Christmas tree.

"See what?"

"The chocolate fountain in the window of Louanne's Homemade Candy Shoppe. It was surrounded by strawberries and pretzels and a whole bunch of other goodies. I'm definitely going to visit that store before I leave."

"You and every other woman in this town." He glanced at the popular shop and drove another block.

Arden laughed suddenly and pointed out her window. "Fit To Be Dyed Beauty Shop. Is that where little old ladies go to get their hair tinted Easter-egg blue?"

Brandon huffed out a laugh. He couldn't help it. Her quirky sense of humor appealed to him. He was almost sorry to reach their destination. Howard and Son's Garage was across the street from the salon. He parked, turned off the engine and opened his door.

Arden placed her hand on his arm and stopped him from getting out. Her skin was warm and soft and awakened feelings in him he'd rather remained dormant. He'd never responded that way to such an innocent touch. "You don't need to go in with me. You must have a hundred things to do."

That was true, yet he wanted to insist on accompanying her. But why should he? John was totally trustworthy. Joni had already volunteered to pick her up when she was finished. Not only that, Arden wasn't his responsibility. He wasn't going to fall back into the habit of rescuing women. Hadn't he just been thinking he needed to maintain his distance? Becoming more involved in her life and her problems was the total opposite of that.

He nodded and restarted the truck, forcing himself to drive off the minute she stepped onto the sidewalk. He needed to get a grip, and fast.

Arden stepped into the building and looked around. A black leather couch that had seen better days was pushed against a windowless wall, a glass coffee table covered with magazines inches in front of it. The smell of oil and brake fluid filled the air. Clanging sounds mingled with Bruce Springsteen, and a howling noise that almost sounded like singing came from the back of the shop.

She crossed the empty waiting room to the laminate counter that divided it from the work area. There was a small silver bell on the counter and she gave it a good ring. A few moments later the noise stopped and the volume on the Springsteen song was lowered.

"Hi. How can I help you?"

She glanced up into smiling brown eyes in a round tan face. "Are you John?"

"In the flesh." He wiped his hands on a stained rag, then shoved the cloth into the pocket of his blue-striped coveralls. He leaned against the counter and swiped a yellow sucker from a bowl. "My wife insisted I give up smoking when she was pregnant with our first child. Now I'm hooked on these."

Arden laughed. "Brandon sent me."

"Ah, so you're Arden."

She nodded and looked longingly at the candy.

He slid the bowl across the counter. "Help yourself. I buy them by the gross. I haven't had a chance to get to your car yet. Emma Johnson's daughter had her baby a month early, so she needs to get to Tennessee as soon as possible to help out. There's no way I could let her hit the road without checking her car first. It's a good thing I did. She needed new brakes and a tune-up. I have a couple more cars to get to, so I might not get to yours for a bit."

"Okay." Arden was astonished by how easily he spilled another person's business. She hoped he wouldn't be as free with her information as he was with this Emma person's.

"Is my car in the back?"

"Yep." He chewed his sucker, then tossed the stick into a trash can.

"I need to get some things out."

"Sure. I need the keys from you anyway."

He grabbed a couple more suckers before leading her to her car. They passed a small office. A pink dollhouse and large cardboard building blocks were squeezed beside a cluttered desk. "Every once in a while I have to bring my kids with me. Toys keep them out of trouble. If not, there's always Attica."

"Attica? Like the prison?"

He nodded toward a folded playpen. "They hate that thing. Can't much say I blame them."

Arden grinned and followed him through the work area and out a steel door. Her Beetle was parked in a small paved lot between a late-model Cadillac and a classic Mustang. After retrieving her overnight bag, she dropped the keys into the mechanic's hand.

"Don't worry. I'll take good care of her."

"Thanks." She left the garage and paused outside, not sure where to go. Her cell phone rang and she set down her suitcase. Arden glanced at the screen and groaned. Jax. No doubt she was on speakerphone. She knew Jax would do all the talking, but Blake would be listening. Her brothers meant well, but they were smothering her and driving her crazy by being so overprotective.

"Hello." She sounded calm and mentally patted herself on the back.

"Where are you? You were supposed to call last night. The hotel in Virginia said you checked out yesterday morning."

"I'm fine, Jackson. There's no need for you to worry."

"Of course there is. You finally broke up with that no-good bum. Instead of turning to Blake or me, you go halfway across the country."

She pulled her suitcase over to a black iron bench and sat. This could take a while, so she might as well be comfortable. "Florida is on the same side of the country."

"You know what I mean."

She did. He wanted her to stay in Baltimore where they could wrap her up in cotton balls to keep her from getting hurt. If they could, they'd keep her from having problems, which in essence was keeping her from having a life. Barring that, they wanted to jump in and solve them for her. That was part of the reason she needed to get away. It would be too easy for her to fall back into her old ways and lean on them instead of standing on her own two feet. She'd never gain their respect if she continued to let them bail her out. She was willing to admit she had played a part in their relationship becoming unequal. If it was to change, she knew she had to do things differently.

"Since you haven't made it to Florida yet, why don't you just turn around and come home?"

And run the risk of seeing Michael-the-pig? Not for a lifetime supply of chocolate-covered pecans. "No."

There was a long pause and she could just envision them whispering furiously as they plotted their next move. Heaven help her from meddling brothers. A bird flew down from its perch in the tree and landed on the edge of a flowerpot overflowing with purple, orange, red and yellow blooms. The wind blew and the scent of the flowers filled her nostrils and she sighed. The bird turned at the sound, then hopped into the flower bed where it began digging in the dirt, perhaps looking for a worm.

"We want to help."

Her brother's voice pulled her attention away from the bird and back to her situation. "I know you do. And I love you both for it. I just need space."

"We understand that. But we need to know you're okay."

She blew out a breath. Just because she was ready to cut the apron strings didn't mean they were. But she was willing to take baby steps to help them along. At least for now. "I'll call you every Sunday."

"And Wednesday."

"No way. Once a week is enough." She had to draw a line somewhere.

There was another long silence, until Jax finally said, "Okay. But you'll call if you need anything—"

This was becoming ridiculous. "Yeah. Sure. Bye."

"Bye. We love you, Arden."

She ended the call and returned her phone to her purse. All things considered, that had gone better than expected. She was finally making strides, no matter how small, in getting her brothers to see her as an adult.

Standing, Arden wheeled the suitcase behind her, curious to see more of the town in the light of day. She'd gone only one block when she came upon Brandon's restaurant. A redbrick building with large windows and purple-and-yellow flowers in pots on either side of the gold-trimmed glass door, Heaven on Earth had a welcoming look. For a moment Arden hesitated, then tried the knob. It turned under her hand. She didn't need to check in with Brandon, but she owed him the courtesy of keeping him abreast of the status of her car. After all, she was a guest in his home.

The dining area was empty, but she figured he must be around. Leaving her suitcase inside the main entrance, she walked through the maze of tables until she stood outside his office. Hearing his voice, she realized he was not alone and had turned to go when a woman's voice stopped her.

"I hate to leave you shorthanded with the rehearsal dinner and reception coming up. I know how important they are to you, Brandon. But I have to go home. My great-aunt raised me and there's nobody else to care for her after her stroke."

"Of course you do. Family is important. Don't worry about work. I'll handle it."

"But you're already short two waitresses. You'll really be in a mess."

"We'll be fine. Is there anything I can do to help?"

"No. I'm set. I didn't have much to pack."

Arden heard paper rustling. "Here's your last check. I've also included a reference letter."

"Thanks. I've been so worried, I didn't even think of that."

"I want you to know, if you decide to return to Sweet Briar, you'll always have a job here."

"I can't even think that far ahead. I'll never forget you. Would you please tell everyone bye for me and that I'll be in touch when I can?"

"Absolutely. And if you need anything, just call."

"Thanks."

The young woman left the office and brushed past Arden, wiping tears as she hurried through the restaurant. Arden hesitantly knocked on Brandon's open door. He was sitting at his desk filling out a form. Pen in hand, he looked up. When he saw her he smiled and leaned back in his chair. Her pulse began to race. What was it about this man that rang her chimes? If she wasn't careful she'd forget she wasn't interested in men anymore.

"I hope I'm not interrupting."

He shook his head and waved her in. "Have a seat."

"Thanks. I met with John. He's not sure he'll be able to get to my car today. I hate to impose on you and Joni another night, so maybe I should get a room at one of the hotels you mentioned."

"That's not necessary. You're not an imposition. You're welcome to stay as long as you need."

"I appreciate that. I couldn't help but overhear your conversation a minute ago."

"With Nora?"

"The waitress?" At his nod she continued. "I know you have a couple of important jobs coming up. I'd love to help if I can."

"You wouldn't by any chance have experience as a waitress, would you?" He sounded as if he was half-joking.

"Actually, I do. I worked as a waitress in a four-star restaurant my last two years of college." Although her family was wealthy, her parents wanted Arden and her brothers to know the value of work. They'd seen too many rich kids living off their trust funds, burning through money they hadn't earned. *A perfect waste of a strong back* was how her father referred to them. Determined that his kids weren't going to become spoiled and lazy, Winston Wexford insisted that his children have summer jobs while in high school. They'd also been required to work part-time while in college. He paid tuition, room and board, and other necessities. Arden and her brothers had paid for any extras they wanted.

Although they each had a sizable trust fund, her father controlled the funds until their thirtieth birthdays, when he expected them to have learned how to be contributing members of society. They received regular generous payments, but, like her brothers, Arden prided herself on making her own way.

"Really?"

She nodded. "Yes. So if you need help I'm willing."

"I appreciate it. Joni usually fills in when I need a waitress, but she's a member of the wedding party. How about you come in tonight and work a shift so you can get a feel for things? I'll pay you, of course."

"You don't need to pay me. I am staying in your house after all."

"Doesn't matter. You'll be paid. If you have a couple of minutes now, we can go over a few things to get you oriented."

Arden followed Brandon out of the office, watching as he moved confidently through the kitchen. He showed her around the spotless room, his pride evident in his every word, before leading her to the dining room.

Although she tried to focus, she was distracted by the play of his muscles under his shirt. His shoulders were broad, his chest well-sculpted, but it was his back that was most interesting to her. The muscles there were strong and flexed as he moved a chair out of the way.

When the tour was over, they returned to his office. He smiled and butterflies began fluttering in her stomach. He might not know it, but his grin was a lethal weapon.

"So, you still interested?"

"Absolutely."

"Good. Let's take care of the paperwork."

"Paperwork?"

"Yes. I want to be able to pay you properly."

She couldn't fill out anything. He'd need a copy of her driver's license. And then he'd know her last name. She hated to think that he would change once he knew who she was, but she'd seen it too many times to believe differently. Money changed people. But she still wanted to help him. Joni had told her this reception was a big opportunity for him, and she didn't want him to look bad simply because he needed more waitresses. She blew out a breath and inspiration hit her. "Do you pay Joni?"

"No. She's pretty hardheaded and won't let me. She does keep her tips, though."

"Then I'll take the same deal Joni has. No salary and I'll keep my tips." She didn't need the money, after all. And he did need the help.

"That's ridiculous. You can't work without pay."

"Why not? You aren't charging me rent. If you insist on paying me, I'll have to pay rent. Either that or I'll move out. Since the bed-and-breakfasts are full, and my car is in the shop and I have no way of getting to one of the hotels you mentioned, I'll probably end up sleeping on a park bench." She was playing dirty, but she wanted to help. She hadn't been raised to be a taker. She needed to pull her own weight.

He opened his mouth and she knew he was going to continue to argue. She cut him off. "That's the deal. Take it or leave it."

He frowned with displeasure and ran a frustrated hand down his face. "I guess I'll take it."

Chapter Four

Brandon plated the seared sesame tuna, and expertly added the side dishes, dipping sauce and wasabi paste, thus finishing the order for table seven. He gestured to the waitress, who grabbed the tray and hustled into the dining area of the restaurant.

The crowd was unexpectedly large for a Tuesday night. He knew part of the reason was all the visitors in town for the wedding. Ordinarily he would be thrilled with the turnout, but tonight he was concerned because of his newest waitress. He didn't want poor service to result in a less-than-spectacular dining experience for his guests, new and regular alike. Great food was only a portion of what Heaven on Earth offered.

True, Arden had experience, but every restaurant had a different way of operating. Although he'd given her a quick orientation, he didn't expect her to remember everything the first night. It generally took at least a week before the waitstaff met his expectations. Of course he had no idea how long she intended to stay in Sweet Briar or if she was interested in working for him on a long-term basis. He'd just be grateful if she stayed through the reception and didn't do any harm to his restaurant's reputation in the process.

Brandon turned his attention back to work. The next hour flew as he prepared dinners quickly yet carefully, ensuring each one was cooked perfectly and attractively presented. Once things slowed down, he went into his office, stripped off his stained whites and put on a navy suit jacket. He removed his hairnet and adjusted the leather strap holding his dreadlocks in place.

He visited the dining room at least once each night. As owner, Brandon wanted his patrons to know he valued them and appreciated their business. More than that, he wanted their feedback. If there was a problem with the food or the service, he wanted them to tell him, not their Facebook friends or Yelp.

He stood at the entrance to the dining room for a moment soaking in the sight and the sounds of his restaurant. The pale gray walls and bluish gray floor-to-ceiling curtains provided the perfect backdrop to the snow-white tablecloths and napkins. The silver-and-crystal chandeliers gave off just the right amount of light to be flattering and cozy at the same time. The soft background music added ambience, but didn't interfere with the quiet conversations his patrons were having.

Satisfied that all was well, Brandon stepped into the dining area. His eyes immediately found Arden. Several diners were scooted to one side of a table and she was taking their picture. She saw him and her face lit up.

His pulse leaped and his blood pounded in his veins. He cursed under his breath. No way was he getting caught under her spell. He brushed a hand over the scars his jacket covered. His days of trusting women were in the past. The last time he'd put his faith in a woman he'd barely escaped with his life. A woman could pass a lie-detector test and he still wouldn't believe a word she said. Not anymore.

"You're in luck," Arden told the patrons, still holding his gaze captive. "The chef is in the dining room. Perhaps he'll pose for a picture with you."

As one, the group of eight people turned and looked at him expectantly. Even though taking pictures did not come close to the top hundred things he wanted to do each day, he'd long since accepted it as part of the job. For a reason that still escaped his comprehension, his guests loved being photographed with him. Apparently, it made the dining experience even more special.

Holding back a sigh, he took his place among the men who were standing behind their seated dates. After Arden snapped a few photos—which she showed to the women, who cooed appreciatively—he shook hands and chatted briefly with them. Each person raved about their meal and the service, promising to return soon and to tell their friends about their experience.

As he crossed the room to greet other diners, he caught another glimpse of Arden. She was the one who should have been photographed. Even in the waitress uniform of a white blouse and straight black skirt, she was absolutely stunning.

Her haircut wasn't traditional, but the short waves were extremely sensual. He'd always liked long hair, believing it was more feminine. Of course, since he now wore his hair long, perhaps he should change his way of thinking. On Arden, he loved the way her hairstyle allowed him to see her face. And what a face it was.

Her brown eyes were warm, revealing an inner kindness. Having seen her face washed clear of makeup he knew her light brown skin was truly flawless and not the result of artfully applied makeup. But it was her quick smile and general openness that appealed to him most, drawing him in even as he did his best to resist.

He dragged his eyes from Arden and continued to work his way around the room. Leah, one of his veteran waitresses, grabbed his arm and steered him to a nearby table where a couple in their forties sat, holding hands and gazing into each other's eyes. "This is Chuck and Valerie Harris. They're celebrating their twentieth anniversary."

Brandon shook the man's hand and smiled at the woman. "Congratulations. I'm honored that you chose to celebrate here."

"My wife and I heard so many things about your restaurant we just had to try it."

"I hope we lived up to your expectations."

"Our meals were perfect and the service was outstanding. Now we know why everyone was raving about this place."

Brandon smiled again. "I never get tired of hearing that. Have you ordered dessert?"

"Not yet," Mrs. Harris said. "I've narrowed it down to three choices, but I can't make up my mind."

"Get them all. Eat one now and take the other two for later as an anniversary gift from us to you."

"Are you sure?" Mrs. Harris asked, beaming.

"Positive." He glanced back and forth between the two. "Again, have a happy anniversary."

He spoke with a few more customers, posed for one more picture, then returned to the kitchen, his favorite place in the world. The next hours sped by as he prepared a variety of perfect meals.

Finally the night ended and the last patrons left, happy sighs trailing them out the door. The waitstaff punched their time cards and then left, calling goodbye as they went.

He'd offered Arden a ride home, which she'd eagerly accepted. He told himself it only made sense as she was currently sleeping in his guest room and not because he wanted to spend time alone with her. She watched him now with a quizzical expression.

"You can wait in my office if you like. Matt has to clean in here and I need to sanitize the kitchen. It won't take long, okay?"

Arden's gaze went to Matt, Brandon's young dishwasher and custodian, who was busy clearing tables. The teen was placing the centerpieces on a serving tray, tossing stray silverware in a bin, then bundling the tablecloths and napkins together. He moved quickly and efficiently.

"I'll help Matt."

"You don't have to do that."

"I know, but there's no sense in sitting around when there's work to be done."

She saw surprise and approval in Brandon's eyes before he turned and left the dining room. Ordering herself not to stare after him, Arden approached the young man. "Want some help?"

"Waitresses don't clean up."

"I won't tell if you don't."

"Sure. As long as you don't mess up. It'll take twice as long if I have to go behind you to fix your mistakes."

He was so serious Arden had to swallow a smile. "Tell me what you want me to do. And how."

He gave such elaborate instructions it was clear he believed his job cleaning the dining room was more important than Brandon's job of preparing the food. The teen watched her clear a table of four, hovering like a mother hen and ready to pounce at the first sign of a mistake. When she finished he nodded, satisfied she wouldn't mess it up too badly. "You can put the tablecloths and napkins on the bench in the entry so Brandon can take them to be laundered."

"Okay."

Matt grabbed a vacuum cleaner and set to work on the floor, laboring over each square inch as if *dirt* was another word for *sin*. Well, cleanliness was next to godliness. She laughed at her own wit, then got back to work. They had just finished when Brandon returned, his stained chef's jacket draped over his arm. He bundled it along with the linens into a laundry bag.

"It looks great in here." He clapped Matt on the shoulder. "Good man."

"Arden helped," Matt mumbled, shuffling his feet, yet standing a bit taller. Obviously Brandon's praise meant a lot.

"I hardly did anything. Besides, you showed me what to do."

Matt flashed a grin that disappeared quickly and he pulled on a gray hoodie. "I'd better get going. Mom has to get up early for work, but she won't go to bed until I'm home." Brandon grabbed the bag of laundry and set the alarm. The three of them stepped outside and Matt headed for a bicycle leaning against the side of the building. A moment later he was pedaling down the moonlit street.

The wind blew and the silver chimes dangling in the trees tinkled. Although the day had been warm, the ocean breeze cooled the town at night. Arden wished she had thought to bring a sweater. She folded her arms across her chest in a futile attempt to ward off the chilly air.

"Cold?" Brandon asked. He was so near she felt his warm breath on her cheek. Her stomach imitated a carnival ride and looped the loop.

"Not really." The wind gusted again, harder this time, and she shivered. "Well, maybe a little."

He slipped off his suit jacket and draped it over her shoulders.

She closed her eyes briefly, indulging in the comfort of that simple gesture. His jacket was still warm from his body and when she inhaled, his clean, musky scent surrounded her and she sighed.

Her eyes popped open. Was she crazy? Back in Baltimore, she'd just been misled and betrayed by a man who on the outside appeared to be a perfect gentleman. But her experience with Michael-the-weasel had turned out to be worse than finding gunk on the bottom of her favorite shoes. She wasn't going to be so gullible again. Just because Brandon was gorgeous and smelled so good didn't mean she had to go and do something stupid like fall for him. She was on a man-free diet.

Brandon dropped the bag of linen into the back of his truck, then opened the passenger door for her. Despite reminding herself of the need to embrace the single life-style, her heart beat a mean pitter-patter at his nearness. Trying not to flutter her eyelashes, she smiled graciously and climbed into the truck, then used the seconds it took him to circle the car and get in to mentally shake some sense into herself.

As he pulled out of the parking lot and into the street, her mind searched for something to distract her from the man beside her. Perhaps conversation would help tamp down her attraction. "Tell me about Matt."

Brandon glanced over at her and smiled. "Matt was my first employee."

"Really? But I thought your restaurant was three years old. No way is that kid a day over seventeen."

"Sixteen. Matt started hanging around a few days after Justin and I started building the restaurant."

"Who's Justin?"

"He and I were partners. I bought him out a couple of months ago. Anyway, Matt was thirteen at the time and begged me for a job. I brushed him off and told him to come back when he was sixteen."

Brandon shook his head at a memory he clearly found amusing. "He showed up the next day saying he was ready for work. He'd come equipped with a broom that was more stick than straw and started sweeping the walk in front of the building. I shooed him away and told him to come back in three years. The next morning I got to work shortly after dawn. Believe it or not, the kid was already there. He was washing the pane window with Windex and a ratty T-shirt."

"Impressive."

"I thought so. I couldn't hire him to work in the res-taurant, but I told him he could run errands for me with a parent's permission. He returned the next day with his mother. She thanked me profusely for hiring her son. Apparently, her husband had run out four years earlier, leaving her to raise Matt and his two younger siblings on her own. While Matt grabbed a broom and kicked up a cloud of dust, his mother confided that the family was barely staying afloat. Matt had been picking up odd jobs, giving his mother all of his earnings."

"And you hired him to do jobs you could have done on your own."

Brandon shrugged. "It was nothing."

Maybe not to him. She was sure it was a big deal to Matt and his family who needed the cash. And Brandon had taken Arden into his home without a second thought. True, she had the money to take care of herself, but money wouldn't put a roof over her head when there was no room in the inn. He'd just stepped in and helped. If she wasn't careful she would start thinking of Brandon as a real-live hero.

"When he turned sixteen I hired him to work in the restaurant. He's probably the best employee I've ever had." He looked at her and winked. "Well, besides you, that is."

She laughed. "Of course."

Brandon pulled the car into the driveway. It felt so natural to walk by his side at the end of the day. Was it only yesterday that her car had broken down and he'd rescued her, welcoming her into his home? She felt so close to him, so comfortable with him, they could have known each other all of their lives. And now, she couldn't imagine her life without him.

Arden peered into the restaurant's dining room. Over the past couple of days she'd worked the lunch shift once and the dinner shift three times. At first she worried that Brandon was giving the opportunity to work to her instead of someone who might actually need the money. She was relieved to discover that wasn't the case. Apparently, he had a hard time keeping waitresses and actually needed her help. That made her feel better about accepting his continuing hospitality. This was a fair trade with each giving something the other needed.

Tonight the restaurant was closed for Carmen and Trent's wedding rehearsal dinner. The bride had chosen purple and teal as her wedding colors and the dining room was decorated accordingly. The usual white napkins had been replaced with blue-green ones. The beautiful centerpieces were comprised of flowers ranging from the palest lilac to the deepest violet. Light flickering from the numerous candles around the room bounced off the softly lit crystal chandeliers. She had never seen a more romantic setting.

She sighed.

"Do I even want to know what that sigh means?" Brandon asked, startling her. He moved incredibly silently for such a large man.

Telling herself her heart was racing because she'd been surprised and not because of the gorgeous specimen standing an arm's length away, Arden brushed a hand over her black skirt, removing imaginary lint. "Sometimes a sigh is nothing more than a sigh. Like the song 'As Time Goes By' says."

He met her gaze, mischief dancing in his dark eyes. *"Casablanca."*

"I know. I love Bogart."

"Do you? The Movie Box Theater in Willow Creek is having a Bogart film festival on Sunday."

"I know. I saw the ad in the newspaper. It sounds like great fun." She tried to control the yearning in her voice, but she heard it.

"It's the day after the wedding. If you're still in town you should go."

"I'll still be here. Unfortunately, my car still won't be fixed. John is still waiting on a part." She grinned. "You weren't kidding about this place being like the Hotel California."

"You itching to leave?"

"Not really," she said, and amazingly it was the truth. There was something about Sweet Briar that appealed to her. The town was beautiful, the citizens friendly and, best of all, no one knew she was a Wexford.

Brandon nodded and rubbed his hand over his chest. He seemed to be debating something and she let him take the time he needed. Finally he spoke. "I'm going to the festival. If you want, you can hitch a ride with me."

"Are you sure?" Arden asked, noticing that Brandon looked as surprised as she felt and guessed he'd shove the words back into his mouth and swallow them if he could. Although he continued to be cordial and friendly, he was maintaining a distance that he hadn't when she first arrived. She couldn't quite put a finger on exactly why he was different, though. Perhaps his reticence was because she was his occasional employee and he wanted to be sure not to cross a line. Whatever the reason, he seemed to be fighting to not be the warm, charming man he was the day they'd met.

"Yep. It's not a big deal."

"In that case, it's a date." Her eyes flew to his and she sputtered. "I don't mean a *date* date."

"I know what you mean," he assured her, stepping

back and once more raising a wall between them. "Now let's get to work."

She watched him walk away, looking for all the world like he regretted asking her. She considered letting him off the hook, but her heart sank to her toes at the thought. Although he might not really want her around, going out with a man who didn't know who she was held an appeal too good to let go.

Chapter Five

The next day, Arden paused by the front window, watching the arrival of the bridal party. The wedding guests had arrived about forty-five minutes earlier and had been dining on finger food and sipping wine while they awaited the bride and groom. There was an excited buzz that had started as a low hum but increased in volume and intensity with each passing moment. The couple's imminent arrival filled the room with anticipation. Disposable cameras had been placed on the tables, and Arden had taken several photographs of the guests as they laughed and posed in small groups, capturing moments the official photographers would have missed.

A white limousine pulled up to the curb in front of the restaurant and someone called out that the bride and groom had arrived. A hush settled over the room as people grabbed their phones and cameras to get good shots of the newly wedded couple as they entered the dining room.

The excitement was contagious. Arden peered out the window again as she hurried to get more bottles of champagne. The chauffeur opened the door and the tuxedoed groom emerged, then reached inside to assist his bride. Dressed in a long white gown covered with beads and lace, Carmen looked like a princess. As she gazed up at her new husband, she smiled and seemed to glow. Arden had never believed love was a visible thing, but in that moment she realized she'd been wrong. She could practically see the love between them. It was as if a sparkly, glistening cord joined the two of them together.

She'd once believed she was in love, but it had been nothing like what she saw between the couple posing for pictures outside the restaurant. Michael-the-creep had never looked at her with the love that was lighting Trent's eyes as he gazed at Carmen. Truth be told, the only time Michael-the-louse had looked that happy was when he was discussing the house he wanted to buy for them, with her money. Or the car... Or any other thing he thought she might like. Of course it would all be purchased with her money. He had been quite clear that he didn't expect her to live off the salary he made as a middle school principal. He'd always said he wanted her to live the life she had been accustomed to. Now she knew the truth. He'd wanted to grow accustomed to that life, as well.

What she hadn't expected was the depths to which he would sink in order to get his hands on her money. That he was willing to make a secret sex tape to try to blackmail her with was bad enough. Worse was finding out that her so-called best friend was in cahoots with him. All her life her parents and brothers had warned her to be careful when choosing friends. She'd really messed up this time. The only saving grace was that she'd found out his plan and left town before he could put it into motion.

The pitiful thing was that she thought she'd learned her lesson about people with her sophomore year roommate in college. Eva had pretended to like Arden and had even insisted on paying her own way when they went to movies and concerts. Arden had thought she'd found a bosom buddy. Overhearing Eva say she'd befriended Arden as part of a plan to land one of Arden's older brothers had really hurt. Even more painful was hearing Eva say it didn't matter whether it was Jax or Blake she ended up with since they were equally capable of buying her everything she wanted.

Thank goodness no one in Sweet Briar knew she had money. She could trust the friendship she'd found with Joni, Brandon and several of her coworkers. As long as no one knew she was an heiress, she would be able to continue to enjoy the relationships she was building.

Arden joined the rest of the staff as a man with a fabulous voice announced the members of the wedding party. She was swept up in the beauty and romance of the moment and her eyes filled with unexpected tears. The joy and love that filled the room was almost too much to take. Blinking fast, she wiped away the tears.

As the bride and groom were finally announced and made their entrance, Arden joined in the applause. She was happy for them, yet a part of her wondered if she would ever find her happily-ever-after.

Arden studied her reflection in the mirror, swirled from side to side and smiled. She'd planned on engaging in some serious retail therapy in Florida, so she'd packed only a couple changes of clothes. The limited wardrobe had worked because most days she was either volunteering at the youth center, helping Brandon at the restaurant or exploring the town. She wanted something more for today's movie festival and had found the perfect outfit in a small boutique across from the diner.

The floral-patterned coral halter dress was perfect for a day at the movies. Fitted at the waist, the skirt flared and hit several inches above her knees. She added three-inch silver sandals and hoop earrings, and the look was complete. Checking her light makeup, Arden glanced in the mirror once more, then scooped her purse from the bed.

There was a knock on her bedroom door. "Ready?"

"Yes," she called. Her heart beat a rapid pitter-patter as she opened the door. Brandon stood in front of her with a sexy grin on his face, looking so good she nearly forgot her name. Both of them. Dressed in faded jeans that hugged his muscular thighs and a lightweight beige top that showed off his incredible upper body, he was the epitome of good-looking male. Definitely Mother Nature had been showing off when she created him. How was a girl supposed to remember she'd sworn off men with Brandon Danielson close enough to touch and smelling like something out of a dream?

"Do you know which movies they're showing today?" Arden asked as they walked to his truck. She mentally patted herself on the back for managing to look at him without her tongue hanging out her mouth.

"I think they're showing *The Maltese Falcon*, *The Big Sleep*, *To Have and Have Not* and my favorite, *The Treasure of the Sierra Madre*. There may be one or two others, but I don't recall the titles," Brandon said as he pulled out of the driveway.

"Oh, I hope they show *Sabrina*. I love that movie."

Brandon tsked. "That is such a chick flick."

"It's a romance."

"Only made bearable by the greatness of Bogart."

"I take it you're not a fan of romantic comedy."

"Nope."

She shook her head and feigned sorrow. "That is so sad. I can see you starring in one. You could totally be the hero and win the girl in the end."

"The last thing I'm interested in is being somebody's hero." He rubbed a hand against his chest. She noticed he did that quite often and wondered if he was even aware he was doing it.

"Too bad. You'd be a great one."

He gave a bitter laugh. "Trust me, it's not all it's cracked up to be."

"You sound like you have experience."

"Nope. Turns out I was just a fool."

"And you'd rather not talk about it."

He glanced at her briefly before returning his attention to the road. "You, Arden West, are both gorgeous and smart."

His casual compliment warmed her even as she felt a twinge of guilt for misleading him. Clearly someone— no doubt a woman—had hurt him. Although curious, Arden didn't press for more information. She'd never deliberately make him uncomfortable. "Flattery will earn you a change in subject."

"Thanks."

They drove along for a while in companionable silence. Leafy trees and wildflowers lined the country road. In the distance a small herd of cows grazed lazily and a few horses raced in an open field. The scenery was so peaceful Arden sighed. "It's so beautiful here."

"That it is."

"But, still, you must miss Chicago." Sweet Briar was a nice time-out from her regular life and she was amazed by how much she was enjoying her stay. The people were so welcoming and she fit in so easily it was as if she'd known many of them for much longer than a week. Still, she couldn't imagine living here year-round. She would miss her parents. And as much as they aggravated her, she would miss Jax and Blake, too.

Brandon laughed. "It's not like I've been banished. I go back to visit my family and friends regularly."

"That's not what I mean."

"I know. And, yes, there are things I miss. I miss the energy of the city. I loved all of the little neighborhood theaters showcasing plays by local artists. And there were so many jazz clubs and piano bars. And don't even mention the symphony. No matter what your interests, there's always something to do." He grinned. "Believe it or not, I really miss public transportation. I liked being able to catch the bus or jump on the 'L' to get where I wanted to go without the hassle of driving."

He pulled into the parking lot of the movie theater. It was nearly full so he had to park in the last row. "But still," he continued as he removed the key from the ignition, "there's something to be said about small-town living. Everyone knows everyone else. There are no secrets or hidden agendas. What you see is what you get. People are truly who they seem to be."

Except her. Guilt filled her when she thought of how she hadn't been truthful about her identity. But her secret wasn't harmful to anyone. No one's life would change if they knew her real last name and net worth. The only thing guaranteed to change was how people treated her, which was something she wanted to avoid as long as possible. The oasis she'd found in Sweet Briar would vanish once people knew she was a Wexford.

"Come on." Brandon opened his door. "We don't want to miss anything. And we need popcorn."

"With extra butter."

"Is there any other way?" he asked, holding out his hand to her. She took it.

"I can't remember the last time I had this much fun."

They were sitting at an old-fashioned ice-cream parlor on the outskirts of Willow Creek Brandon thought she would enjoy. Arden dragged her tongue over her orange sherbet, dabbing at a drip on her cone. His stomach clenched in response. Eating his chocolate ice cream didn't give him nearly as much pleasure as watching her eat her dessert.

"You're only saying that because they showed your chick flick."

She gave a delectable little giggle as she took another taste. "I like happy endings. There aren't enough of those in life."

"Are you looking for yours?"

"Not anymore. I'm through with men. My life is more of a horror story than a romance."

"You're young. This is only the beginning. You don't know what's going to happen in the middle or how your story is going to end."

"The credits don't have to roll for me to know what kind of movie I'm in. It's definitely not a romance." She finished her cone, wiped her mouth with a napkin and tossed it into the garbage, flashing him a smile. "Maybe my life is a mystery."

"That's better than horror, I suppose."

"Or slapstick. I would hate to get a pie in the face. I don't think that would be much fun."

"Trust me, it's not."

"Are you speaking from experience?"

"Unfortunately."

She leaned her chin into her hand. "This sounds interesting."

He tossed his napkin into the trash and dusted his hands on his jeans. He looked around the parlor. They were the only customers left and the waiter was leaning against the bar, alternately looking at the giant clock on the wall and throwing dirty looks in their direction. "We should leave so he can close."

She stood and followed him. "No way you're getting out of telling me what happened."

He waited until they were on the road home before telling her the story. "It wasn't exactly pie in the face. It was crème brûlée tossed on my chef whites by an irate waitress."

"Wow. I wouldn't have had the nerve. What did you do?"

"What could I do? I wiped off my clothes and kept cooking. After I fired her."

She tossed him a mischievous grin. "No. I mean what did you do to make her throw dessert at you?"

"Nothing. I just expected her to do her job. She preferred to go on a hot date with a lawyer."

"Ah, romance."

"For him it was probably more like a big-budget disaster movie."

She laughed, her eyes dancing with humor. If he wasn't careful, he could fall for her. That was a sobering thought and the smile died on his lips. He wasn't going to open his heart again no matter how appealing Arden was. Not in this lifetime.

"Thanks again for taking me," she said, pulling him out of his reverie.

"No problem. I enjoyed the company."

"You know, I've been thinking," Arden said as they walked into the house. "You and Joni have been great to let me stay with you, but I should probably move out. John says the part for my car won't arrive until Tuesday, so I'll be in Sweet Briar a couple more days. The last of the wedding guests left town this morning, so I can check into the bed-and-breakfast tomorrow."

He tried to meet her gaze, but she was looking everywhere but at him. Without thinking, he tilted her chin so their eyes met. He saw the surprise and immediately dropped his hand, shoving it into the pocket of his jeans, trying to downplay the electric spark that he'd felt when he touched her face. "Don't you remember? Kristina said she was booked for the summer."

"Right." She frowned and two lines appeared between her eyebrows. A second later they disappeared and a slight smile lifted her full lips. "But she mentioned that other place."

"The Come On Inn?"

She nodded. "I can try to get a room there."

"You can try. Call them in the morning to see what is available if that's what you want to do." His heart pinched at the thought of her leaving, which was ridiculous—and proof that he really did need for her to leave his home, if not Sweet Briar. How could he possibly be attached to her? He barely knew her. Sure she was sweet and funny, not to mention beautiful. But so were a lot of women. He had no problem hanging around them when the urge struck him. Nor did he have any difficulty walking away when the time came.

So what made Arden different? Why was the thought of her leaving his home so difficult if not painful? It wasn't, he decided. She was no different from any other woman. He wouldn't allow her to be.

"That's what I'll do."

She smiled at him and the two of them stood as if frozen, which was odd since he was suddenly over-heated. The air between them crackled with electricity and her heady scent swirled around him, enticing him to move closer. The urge to take her into his arms very nearly overcame him. He inhaled and forced himself to remember the danger that came from getting emotion-ally involved with a woman. Normally he was able to separate the physical and the emotional, but he knew he would not be able to do that with Arden. At least not easily. So he muttered good-night and walked away be-fore he did something stupid.

Arden hung up the phone and sighed. There was no room at the Come On Inn. For good measure, she'd con-tacted Kristina at the Sunrise and been told the same thing. Kristina had enthused about having every room booked for the next two months then rambled on in what could only be called free association, talking about ev-erything from the flowers lining the street to spinach salad. She had promised to let Arden know if she had any cancellations.

Not having a room to rent wasn't the worst thing in the world. Far from it. In fact it wasn't the worst news she'd had that day. That news had been delivered bright and early by John. Apparently, there was labor strife at the parts factory and he didn't know when he would receive the part he needed for her Beetle. He'd tried calling around to other suppliers but hadn't been able to get his hands on it. He had no idea when her car would be ready.

At this point, Arden had a decision to make. She could hire a tow truck and return to Baltimore. That thought roiled her stomach. She was not ready to return home and face the situation with Michael-the-peanut-brain. She also wasn't ready to deal with her smothering brothers. Especially not since she was finally able to breathe freely. She needed the distance, which was why she'd been going to Florida in the first place. Going back home wasn't an option.

Hopping a flight and going to her parents' winter home in Florida had also lost its appeal. She no longer wanted to spend her days alone in that big house while her parents traveled through Europe. She no longer craved the solitude.

She could remain in Sweet Briar. Brandon had said she could stay with him and Joni until her car was ready. Of course at the time they'd all believed it would be only a day or two, three at the most. Surely he wouldn't have made such a generous offer had he known it would be open-ended. She didn't want to become the houseguest who wouldn't leave.

She could always go somewhere else, but Sweet Briar

was growing on her. It had taken only a couple of days to discover why this place had become a tourist destination. There were so many cute shops to explore, fun places to visit and, of course, the beach. This was a wonderful place for a vacation.

More than that, the people were warm and welcoming, making her want to stay. Unlike the Hotel California, she didn't want to check out. She definitely wasn't ready to leave. She could envision spending a few more weeks here. But she had to find another place to stay.

She didn't feel right staying in Brandon's home. There was something very intimate about that. And the more she was around him, the more attracted she became. He was unlike any man she'd ever met. Sure, he was strong and hardworking. But, more than that, he gave his best in everything and expected others to do the same. His high standards and belief in others inspired them to give their all.

How could she help but admire him? She couldn't. Which was why she needed to put some physical distance between them so she could maintain her emotional distance.

Joni seemed to know everyone and she had her finger on the pulse of this town. If anyone had a place for rent, she would know.

Slipping her phone into her pocket, Arden headed for the youth center. Over the past few days she had spent many hours volunteering there. She was quite impressed with Joni and what she managed to do on a shoestring budget. The place was filled with kids of all ages engaged in a variety of activities. A group of young teenage girls walked slowly by two older boys. One of the boys smiled and the other said hello. The girls burst into giggles and hurried away.

Arden shook her head and bit back a smile.

"Ah, young love."

Arden turned at the sound of Brandon's voice. "What are you doing here?"

He held up a round tray with a clear plastic cover. "One of the kids is having a birthday today and Joni needed cupcakes."

She looked closer at the treats. "You baked them?"

"Perish the thought. I stopped at Polly Wants A Cookie and picked them up for her. What are you doing here?"

"Looking for Joni. I was hoping she knew of a place I can rent for a couple of weeks."

"Oh."

She couldn't tell what that one word meant, but a crazy part of her hoped it was disappointment that she wouldn't be staying in his guest room any longer. That thought only proved that she was losing her mind and that she needed to put distance between them.

"Yes. There's some sort of labor dispute at the place where the part for my car is being manufactured. Long story short, John doesn't know when he'll be able to fix my car so I need to find a place to stay. Joni knows everyone so…" Arden's voice trailed off as she realized that Brandon was staring mutely as she babbled. She clamped her jaw shut, refusing to let another word escape.

"Did I hear you say you were looking for a place to stay?" Joni asked from behind Arden, making her jump. She'd been so entranced by Brandon that she hadn't heard the other woman approach.

"Yes." She quickly summarized her conversation

with the mechanic. "Since you know everyone, I figured you might have a lead on a room I can rent."

"You know you can stay in the house."

"Three days for fish and houseguests. Any longer and they start to smell. I've been in your house for a week. I don't want you to hold your nose when you see me."

Joni laughed. "I get your point although I don't agree. But I can do better than a room. Brandon and I have a garage apartment. It's renovated and just sitting empty. You're welcome to stay there as long as you need. Isn't that right, Brandon?"

Arden's eyes flew to his. His poker face was firmly in place but he nodded. After a long moment he replied, "Sure."

"I don't want to impose."

"You're not imposing," Joni replied before he had a chance.

"If you're sure." Arden glanced at Brandon again.

He nodded, but a part of her wondered if he really was envisioning strangling his sister. "Stay as long as you need."

"Thanks."

He handed the tray of cupcakes to his sister. "I need to get going. I'll catch up with you two later."

Brandon was gone so fast Arden didn't have a chance to thank him for his continued hospitality. "Are you sure it's okay? Brandon seems kind of reluctant."

"Positive." Joni juggled the tray of pink-iced cupcakes. "Do you have time to hang out for a while? I need to set up a party for one of our little girls, then I'll be available to show you the apartment in about an hour."

"Sure. If you need an extra hand, I have two."

"I always need help."

Arden helped Joni decorate a room for the party. They draped streamers from the ceiling and taped some on the walls. Next they blew up blue and green balloons and bundled them into centerpieces they placed on the paper tablecloths covering the long table. They blew up pink balloons and tied them to the back of the gray folding chairs. Finally they hung up a colorful banner, then stood back to admire the festive room.

"Impressive, if I do say so myself," Joni said, folding the step stool and carrying it to the closet.

"I agree, but not only about the room. I mean you. I didn't know youth centers hosted birthday parties." Arden would have smiled, but blowing up balloons was hard on the jaws. They needed a helium tank something fierce.

Joni closed the door and leaned against it. "We're an all-purpose center. Sweet Briar is prospering, but there are still some families that are struggling. We try to help out when we can. Like the party for this girl. Her mother has cancer and is fighting to live. The father is not in the picture."

"Hence the party."

"Yes."

Arden followed Joni from the room, her mind busy. She wanted to make a donation to the youth center to help them continue their good work. Because she wanted to maintain her anonymity, she wouldn't be able to make the gift until she returned home. But she didn't want to wait. They could do even more good if they had the funds. She would contact her brothers and convince them to give, as well. They were always supporting worthy causes and she couldn't think of one more deserving than the youth center.

Arden and Joni chatted nonstop on the ride to the apartment. Joni ran into the house for the keys, then met Arden outside the garage. Arden followed Joni up the flight of stairs, holding her breath until she opened the door.

"It's beautiful," Arden said as she stepped inside and looked around.

"Do you think you'll be comfortable here?"

"Definitely." Arden ran her hand across the black granite breakfast bar that separated the kitchen from the living room, then straightened one of the three stools with black-and-white-striped cushions that comprised the dining area. The living room was quaint with a cream love seat and matching chair with gray, black and red decorative throw pillows. A small bookcase overflowed with a variety of paperbacks.

"Okay. It's yours for as long as you want."

"Thanks. Now about rent."

"Arden."

"Joni."

"You're my friend."

"Exactly. Friends don't take advantage of friends."

Joni sighed and named an absurdly low figure. Arden raised her eyebrow and Joni doubled the number.

Arden smiled. "Agreed."

"You drive a hard bargain."

"I just want to do what's fair."

Shaking her head, Joni handed over the key and left. Arden walked through the apartment again, her home for the foreseeable future. Of course, if there was one thing life had taught her, it was that nothing about the future could be foreseen.

Chapter Six

Brandon leaned against the back door and stared across the dark yard. A ribbon of light filtered through the window of the garage apartment. He wondered what Arden was doing. He hadn't seen her since this morning at the youth center when he'd run away like his pants were on fire.

Despite the fact that she'd stayed with them for only a week, he missed her presence. He'd grown accustomed to her easy laughter and quick if somewhat offbeat wit. Her wicked and quirky sense of humor matched his and he found himself relaxing around her. In fact, he felt more at ease with her than he did with anyone besides Joni. The feeling of rightness that filled him whenever they were together caught him off guard and he wasn't sure how to handle it. Thus, the race away from her this morning.

After Sylvia, he'd sworn off relationships, choosing

instead to focus on his restaurant. Sure, he had dated in the past three years, but he was always careful to let the woman know the rules. No hearts were involved under any circumstances. He didn't do love. But dating an endless stream of women, no matter how beautiful or charming they were, had become tiresome and left him empty. Being alone had become preferable.

No woman had attracted his interest until Arden stumbled into his life. She'd already found a way into his mind and was consuming his thoughts. He wasn't ready for anything serious or emotional. What he needed was to reinforce the barrier around his heart before she tunneled her way in there, too.

And now he stood here in his kitchen like some teenager, lurking in the shadows hoping to get a glimpse of the object of his affection. This was pathetic. *He* was pathetic. He needed to get a grip.

"I'm all packed and ready to go," Joni said, sauntering into the room. He spun around, but not fast enough to fool her. She smirked. "My brother, the Peeping Tom."

"I don't know what you're talking about." Could he sound any guiltier?

"Uh-huh. Sure. I can spell it out if you need me to."

"Leave it alone."

She wrapped her arms around him and gave him a tight hug. "Not all women are like Sonya."

"Sylvia. Her name was Sylvia."

"Right. Not that it makes a difference. My point is the same. Not every woman is a liar."

"I never said they were."

"You don't need to. Your actions speak loud and

clear. You never let a woman get close enough to find out what her character is."

"I don't have time for that. I'm concentrating on my restaurant."

"Hiding behind it is more like it."

He pulled out of her embrace and sat at the table. The garage apartment was still visible from his chair and he forced his eyes to look anywhere but there. He should have sat somewhere else. It was too late to switch seats with Joni watching and interpreting his every move. "That's not what I'm doing. I need to work hard so I can succeed."

"You have more than succeeded and you know it."

He shrugged. "Maybe, but you know how tough the restaurant business can be. I have to work hard to keep from growing stale and losing ground. If I want to grow my reputation in the industry, I have to continue to create and innovate. That takes time and energy."

He'd taken out a loan in order to buy out Justin. He was making his payments, but a decline in business would make that difficult. He needed to stay focused on what was important, and that wasn't the woman currently occupying his garage apartment.

"Even if you need to work, you still need to make time for love."

"Love? I finally got the folks off my back and you want to start in? I'll tell you what I told them. I'm not interested in love anymore." He stood to his full height. He always needed every advantage when debating with Joni. "And speaking of love, I don't exactly see you marching down the aisle."

"Touché. Consider the topic closed."

Now that he'd won the argument, he smiled at his sister. "You need a ride to the airport?"

"No. Lex is going to drop me."

"Ah."

"Ah, nothing." Joni hopped to her feet, proving that a good offense was the best defense. "I'd better get some sleep. I have an early flight. But before I go, I need you to do something for me."

"What's that?"

"Look after Arden."

"Joni."

She raised a hand. "I'm just asking you to spend a bit of time with her. She's alone in town with no transportation or friends. I'm going to introduce her around when I get back, but in the meantime, you're all she has. Remember, she just broke off with her boyfriend. Don't let her spend all her time alone in that apartment. Be nice to her. Please."

"Joni. I don't need you matchmaking."

"I'm not. I'm just imagining how I would feel in her shoes."

He shook his head. Joni drew people to her without trying. She would always have friends, new to town or not. But Arden was more reticent than Joni. She didn't seem to make friends as easily as his sister. Knowing he'd been played but unable to fight back, he huffed out a breath and nodded. "I won't leave her alone."

"You'll hang out with her?"

"Didn't I just say that?"

"You're the world's best brother." Joni kissed his cheek then bade him good-night.

When he had the kitchen to himself once more, Brandon wondered why he had agreed. He hoped it was because he shared Joni's compassion. Somehow he didn't think that was the entire reason. Still it was the best he could come up with on short notice.

Brandon sniffed the soup, spooned a bit of it into his mouth, let it settle on his tongue for a few seconds and then swallowed. Frowning, he set the spoon beside the bowl and leaned against the kitchen counter. Something was missing from the new bouillabaisse recipe he was creating, but he couldn't put his finger on it.

One of the things he really enjoyed was putting a new spin on old favorites. Anyone could follow a recipe and make a good meal. It took a special gift to create a dish that people made reservations weeks in advance in order to try. He had that gift.

He took another taste. He wished Joni was around so he could ask her opinion, but she was in Chicago visiting their parents and no doubt getting grilled like a good steak. They wanted grandchildren and none of their three children were cooperating. As the oldest, Russell should have been their target. A career military officer, he was currently stationed outside the United States and safely out of nagging range. After the mess with Sylvia, Brandon's parents were giving him a reprieve. Thankfully, they'd stopped trying to introduce him to the unmarried daughters of their friends. That left Joni the sole focus of their attention. She always took their pressure with a smile in her good-natured way. No doubt she was enjoying her visit and catching up with her friends, coming up with creative ways to avoid countless blind dates with men, each of whom their parents were sure was *the one*.

Still, he wished she was here so she could serve as his taste tester.

A movement outside the window caught his eye. Arden. Dressed in a short denim skirt that showcased her world-class legs and a white T-shirt with a gray design that fit perfectly over her perky breasts, she was skipping down the steps like a young girl. His window was open and he could hear her singing a song he always turned off whenever it came on the radio. His music preferences ranged from jazz and blues to his preferred classical but didn't include pop.

Brandon remembered his promise to Joni. He'd said he wouldn't leave Arden to her own devices until Joni returned. And he did need someone to taste his soup. Before he could change his mind, he called out to her. "Do you have a few minutes?"

She paused, one foot on the bottom step, met his eyes through the screen, then nodded. Even from this distance, he could see the brilliant smile on her face and his body responded. There was just something about Arden that appealed to him on a basic level. Despite knowing it would be better if he kept her at arm's length, part of him longed to draw her closer. And not just physically. Sexual attraction could be easily understood and dismissed. But more than wanting her body, he wanted to know her. He wanted to discover what made her laugh and what upset her. He wanted to hear about her dreams and share his with her. Given the fact that he didn't want to open his heart to anyone, the last thing he should have done was give her a place to stay.

Though she claimed to have sworn off relationships, he knew that vow wouldn't last. She had too much love inside to keep it to herself. Eventually she'd want to share that love with a man and, later, children. She'd want the white picket fence and all the trimmings. Before Sylvia, he'd wanted forever as well, and Arden would have fit into his life perfectly. But he didn't believe in happily-ever-after. Not anymore.

Arden stepped inside the kitchen, bringing with her the happiness and sunshine that followed her around even on the gloomiest day. "Did you need me?"

"Yes." He grabbed a spoon and dipped it into the pot. "Taste this." He held the spoon up to her. Her eyes widened and she hesitated before opening her mouth and then closing her lips over the spoon. She swallowed but didn't say anything.

"Well?"

"Bouillabaisse."

"And?"

She tilted her head. "And what?"

"What do you think?"

"It tastes different somehow. Better."

"I'm trying to create a new recipe but can't figure out what's missing."

"Nothing's missing. It's good."

"But not great."

She laughed and her eyes lit as she looked longingly at the pot. "I think it's great. It's the best I've ever had."

He filled a bowl, offered it to her, then pulled out a chair for her. "Sit down and eat."

"Thanks. I thought you'd never ask." She ate another spoonful of soup, then looked up with her ever-present smile. "So do you do this a lot?"

"Work on new recipes? Every Tuesday. I want to offer the best food to my customers and create new twists on old favorites. That requires work." He rubbed his chin. "Well, not exactly work, but concentration and time."

"It sounds like fun."

"It is."

The spoon disappeared between her perfect lips and she moaned softly. He struggled to keep his imagination under control. She swallowed and he forced himself to refocus his attention on the missing ingredient and not the way her pink tongue flicked against her plump bottom lip.

"How old were you when you decided you wanted to be a chef?"

"Nine."

"Really? I thought boys that age wanted to be athletes or police officers or firefighters."

"Not me. I always knew I wanted to own my own restaurant. My grandfather had a soul-food restaurant. I started hanging out with him when I was about eight. Just a couple of hours a day in the summer and on Saturdays during the school year. I had my own stool in the kitchen where I watched him cook." Brandon folded his arms against his chest, seeing the past so clearly it could have happened only yesterday. "He was something. A genuine artist. His food was phenomenal. Granddad made macaroni and cheese that was so good it made you want to slap your mama."

Arden's laugh was a sweet sound that battered his flagging resistance. She was getting to him.

"And his greens? Please. People came from all over the Midwest for a forkful. He didn't play music in the restaurant because people loved his food so much they sang while they ate. The top choir directors used to get their best inspiration just from eating there."

"You're making that up."

"Exaggerating maybe. But only a little."

"Well, if his food was anywhere near as good as yours, then it had to be great."

"Thanks."

"Did you study cooking in school, too?"

"Yeah. I was the only dude in high school who took home ec. All the other guys were taking wood shop and auto mechanics. I might not be able to rebuild a car engine, but I can make a soufflé that can bring tears to your eyes."

"And bouillabaisse that is so good one bowl isn't enough."

Taking her less-than-subtle hint, he refilled her bowl. "After high school I studied at the CIA."

"You're a spy, too?" she asked, her spoon frozen inches away from her mouth.

He chuckled. She really was cute. "No. The Culinary Institute of America. From there I went to France and later to Italy and Spain to learn."

"Then you came to Sweet Briar to open your restaurant," she said, finishing the story for him.

"Not quite." His cell phone rang and he looked down at the screen. Sylvia. Again. Think of the devil and she'll show up. She'd called him out of the blue three days ago. He'd been shocked to hear her voice after all this time. Before his lungs had filled with his next breath, an all-consuming rage had filled him and he'd told her never to call him again. Clearly she'd chosen to ignore that request. No surprise there. She didn't believe rules applied to her.

She'd cost him his dream and nearly his life, and yet she still had the nerve to track him down. Nothing she could say would ever be of the slightest interest to him. He'd been fooled once, but it wouldn't happen again.

Memories of his time working at a famous Chicago restaurant flashed through his mind, flushing his previous good mood. He'd been close to accomplishing his dream of becoming a nationally known chef when she'd entered his life with her treachery and all but destroyed him. In the end nothing remained of the life he'd mapped out for himself, so he'd moved to Sweet Briar and begun building a new life. A life that didn't include love.

The sudden glacial look in Brandon's eyes puzzled Arden. One moment they were laughing and talking, and then his phone rang. He'd frowned as he looked at the screen but hadn't taken the call. Now the look on his face was cold enough to give her frostbite. A part of Arden told her to leave, but she ignored it. She wanted to know what had made him morph from a charming man into a living, breathing Popsicle. And why pain had flashed in his eyes before he masked it.

"Oh. That's right. You moved from Chicago three years ago. I remember you telling me that. Why did you move here?" She didn't know if the phone call was responsible for the change in his attitude or if talking about his reason for moving to Sweet Briar was the cause, but she was curious about the rest of his story. Maybe hearing it would help her understand why his mood had shifted so radically. And she wanted to understand. "Why move from Chicago, which has some of the best and most famous restaurants in the country, to a small town? You could get way more recognition there. And you deserve it. With your talent you could have your own cooking show and publish bestselling cookbooks."

"I had my reasons."

That answer should have been enough of a hint. Clearly he didn't want to talk about it. A wiser woman would have let it go. She would have, too, if she hadn't seen the pain behind the wall he'd erected and recognized that pain as one she'd experienced herself.

It was the pain of betrayal. Although thinking of Michael-the-turd annoyed her, she didn't hurt with the same intensity as she had when she'd discovered that he was only using her. But she knew now she hadn't been in love. Not really.

Whatever had happened to Brandon must have been truly devastating for him to still feel the ache. And it was clear he was hurting. Not only that, he'd uprooted himself, moving from Chicago, where his career knew no limits, to Sweet Briar. No matter how much praise he received from his customers, his career would never reach the zenith it once could have.

It occurred to her that he was hiding from his life. Something she knew about all too well. Sure, he'd opened a restaurant and continued to create dishes, but his potential was severely limited. Maybe if she pressed, he would talk about it. And maybe, please God, maybe, he would get over the pain. She took a breath and let it out. "I'm sure you do have your reasons. But you have a great gift. An incredible gift. And you're hiding your light under a bushel. Did you really study all those years just to open a restaurant in a town of less than two thousand people?"

He placed both hands on the table and inhaled deeply. When he looked up, she met his eyes and knew she'd made a mistake. He'd been angry before. Now he was furious. "I don't have to explain myself to you."

"I'm not asking for an explanation. It's just that I care. I don't think your grandfather would be happy to see you're not living up to your potential."

Brandon held up his hand, indicating she should stop. "You don't know anything about me, so stop. Now."

"You're right. I'm sorry. I'll leave." Guilt and sorrow filled her. She had wanted to make things better but, instead, had made them worse. Jumping up, she headed for the back door. Blinded by guilty tears, she missed a step and tumbled down two stairs before she was able to grab on to the railing.

"Arden." Brandon materialized, reaching out to her.

She swatted his hand away, ashamed that she'd overstepped. Didn't she hate it when her brothers tried to tell her what to do, like they thought they knew better than she did what was best for her life? And she had done the same to Brandon. "I don't need your help. Thanks. I can make it down the stairs on my own."

"Obviously," he said drily, and moved out of the way.

Straightening, she put weight on her right foot and nearly crumpled. She must have made a sound of pain because he was there in an instant, sweeping her off her feet. Holding her in his arms, he hesitated a moment as if trying to decide what to do with her now that he had her. He shook his head and then climbed the stairs. He strode through the kitchen and down a hall, nudging open a partially closed door to what she guessed was his home office. After shoving books and papers onto the floor, he set her on a butter-soft leather couch.

The room was bright although nothing to write home about. There were piles of cookbooks and magazines on a brown leather chair, the oak table and the floor. In fact, the only surface that wasn't piled with books and papers was the enormous, gleaming desk. It held a phone, a desk calendar and a computer, all of which appeared to be perfectly centered. Interesting. It was as if two people inhabited this one space—one neat and the other incredibly disorganized. Sort of like the evil genius meets his anal twin.

"Let me look at your ankle."

"I'm fine." She tried to pull her leg away, but he grasped her calf firmly. Hot fire shot through her body. She wanted to believe the pain from her ankle caused the reaction, but that would have been the biggest lie ever told. His callused and knife-nicked hands gently holding her foot was responsible for the tingles that wiggled up and down her spine.

"You're not fine. Now hold still. I'm not going to hurt you."

"I know. But I feel like I hurt you. I'm just so embarrassed. I shouldn't have overstepped. I know we've only known each other for a short time, but I feel close to you. Like I know you. But, still, I shouldn't have said what I did. Please, please, please forgive me."

His intense eyes bored into her as if trying to see clear to her soul. She looked away and forced herself to continue, her voice much softer. "I don't have a lot of friends and I thought you could be one. Believe it or not, I was trying to be a friend to you. But I forgot, friends don't step over the line. Especially one so clearly drawn."

"I see."

Arden let the silence go on as long as she could stand.

Was he her friend or not? Did he accept her apology? "Well?"

"I don't think your ankle is broken or even sprained. You just twisted it. I'll get some ice." He placed a couple of throw pillows under her ankle before leaving her alone, his actions speaking more eloquently than any words could. He wasn't interested in being her friend. Her eyes welled and she blinked back tears, determined not to let him see just how deeply his rejection cut.

"This should help," he said as he returned. She turned her head away and swiped at the tear that had escaped, then turned back to him. He squatted beside her and gently placed the towel-wrapped ice on her swelling ankle before meeting her eyes. "And I accept your apology."

That was it? Well, what did she expect? She'd insulted him. Now she had to accept the fallout. She'd ruined something good. She blinked furiously, but another tear escaped and trickled down her face.

"Don't cry."

The kindness in Brandon's voice was her undoing and the tears came faster. It would have been easier to maintain her control if he'd acted like a jerk the way she deserved. But his understanding broke the dam holding back the flood of emotions and sobs she'd refused to shed when she'd learned the truth about her so-called friends back in Baltimore.

He sat on the couch and pulled her into his arms, his masculine scent surrounding her. She didn't resist, but went gratefully, thankful for the comfort.

He brushed his lips across her hair. His hands caressed her back gently. Gradually her tears slowed and the mood in the room shifted. It wasn't a slow shift, but rather a dramatic one. One minute the feel was comforting. The next the room crackled with sexual tension.

She'd found him attractive almost from the first second she'd laid eyes on him. What woman wouldn't? With his handsome face, intelligent eyes and muscular physique, he was sex appeal personified. As she'd gotten to know him, she had discovered that a kind man lived within that gorgeous body.

With her head against his chest, she felt his heartbeat change from slow and steady, the rate increasing until it matched the rapid beat of her own. She lifted her head and searched his eyes. They were so dark that the pupil and iris were nearly the same color. He lifted one corner of his mouth and huffed out what almost passed as a laugh, then lowered his head until his lips almost touched hers. "This is such a bad idea."

"I know." But when he touched her lips with his own she didn't think about turning away.

Kissing her temporary boss and landlord might not be among her brightest decisions, but it was definitely one of the most pleasurable.

Chapter Seven

Brandon heard Arden sigh as she leaned closer. Her soft breasts pressed against his chest, igniting a fire within him. Kissing her broke at least two of his rules, but when she put her arms around his neck and settled more comfortably on his lap, he couldn't remember what they were. He angled his head and deepened the kiss. She tasted of the savory bouillabaisse she'd been eating and her own natural sweetness. The combination was heady and delicious, and his body responded as his desire grew.

The telephone rang, bringing with it his sanity. He didn't look at the screen, letting the call go to voice mail. It was enough to cool him off and help him regain control. He shouldn't be doing this. Arden worked for him, even if only sporadically and despite the fact that she refused to accept payment beyond her tips. In his mind she was his employee, which put any type of physical relationship off-limits. Not only that, she was vulnerable. She might not be mourning the breakup with the jerk, but she'd been hurt recently. The pain was bad enough for her to go chasing across the country for some time away. Only deep hurt could cause such a re-action. He ought to know. With the two violated rules now clear in his mind, he reluctantly set her on the sofa beside him and leaned his forehead against hers.

"I know I should apologize, but to be honest I'm not sorry." Far from it. He wanted to kiss her until she didn't know her own name.

"Why should you be? I was a willing participant." She scrunched up her nose, looking sexier than she should. "Do you apologize to all the women you kiss? I mean, I could see saying you're sorry if you were a rotten kisser, but you're not."

His chest puffed out with pride, which was ridicu-lous. He'd been kissing girls since he was thirteen. With fifteen years of practice he should be good. He brushed a finger across her flushed cheek, then across her lips, which were damp and a bit swollen. "That's not why I'm apologizing. You were upset. I should have considered your state of mind and exercised more self-control."

She shrugged away his concern, then nibbled her bottom lip. "I'm sorry for what I said. I do admire you. But I have no right to try to run your life. I know what that feels like."

He considered her words and admitted to himself that she hadn't been entirely wrong. He had been running from his life when he'd first come to town. He'd been both physically and mentally scarred. But he liked the life he was creating here. "I know. And I believe you spoke from concern and friendship."

"I did. I don't want to be a judgmental know-it-all."

"You're not." He cut her off, knowing she would apologize ceaselessly if he didn't. Anyone could make a mistake. Certainly he had made his share. He rubbed the back of his neck. "Arden, this can't happen again."

"The kiss, you mean?"

"Yes. I shouldn't have done that. I won't do it again."

"What if I kiss you first?"

"Still no."

"Oh, phooey."

He laughed. She was such a determined little thing. But he had rules. He might have considered overlooking the employer/employee rule since she was only temporary, but he wasn't willing to break the most important rule of all: never become involved with a woman with whom he could fall in love. And Arden most assuredly fit into that category. Heck, the category might as well have been made for her. Even now he had to fight the urge to sweep her into his arms and pick up where they'd left off. But he wouldn't want to stop there. And it wasn't just because he desired her physically. He cared for her.

"Can we still be friends?" Her voice sounded small and tentative, almost as if she expected him to say no.

"Yes. We can absolutely still be friends." He just needed to make sure his body understood the meaning of the word and that kissing was not included.

She tilted her head to the side and smiled. "Good. Because outside of my family I don't have very many people in my life I can trust."

He could understand her lack of faith. He could

count on one hand and still have fingers left the number of people he truly trusted who weren't related to him. Somehow she was easing her way into that small circle. As much as he enjoyed holding her and despite how perfectly she fit in his arms or, perhaps, because of it, he needed to establish the necessary distance between them before he did something foolish like let her into his heart.

He rose and shifted the pile of papers and books from a chair to the floor in order to give his hands something to do.

"I should leave so you can get back to what you were doing."

Arden swung her legs around slowly as if trying to avoid bumping her ankle into anything. Brandon knew the sensible thing—the right thing—was to offer her his arm and help her walk out of his house. So naturally he bent and scooped her into his arms.

He expected her to make at least a token protest, but she didn't. Instead, she wrapped her arms around his neck and leaned her head against his shoulder. The warmth from her soft body heated him and he was instantly aroused. Her sweet scent was too delicate to have come from a bottle of perfume. It could have been her shampoo or lotion or any number of things, but he knew it was just Arden. That unique scent that turned him on so much could never be duplicated.

He carried her through the kitchen, down his back stairs, across the lawn and up the stairs to her garage apartment, wishing the distance was farther. She felt so right in his arms. With every step he tried to extinguish his growing desire. It wasn't just physical. That he could handle. What worried him was the part of him that wanted more from Arden. The part that forgot the agony of being burned by a woman's lies. Of being shot and nearly killed because of her deceit. The part that wanted a future.

The rational part of him reasserted itself and he mentally withdrew to a safe distance. He would never make himself vulnerable again. Even with Arden.

Arden stretched, straightened her legs, then immediately winced and sucked in her breath as pain shot through her ankle. Most of the swelling had gone down, but an ache remained.

After Brandon had settled her on the couch, she'd insisted that she would be fine once she'd taken a pain pill. Her ankle was hurting so badly she'd ignored the fact that she was a real lightweight when it came to any type of medicine. One little pill was all it took to knock her out for the afternoon.

She looked at the clock and jerked upright. It was nearly six thirty. After limping to the bathroom she hopped to the kitchen, using the wall and any pieces of furniture she could get her hands on for balance. Although small, the kitchen had all the modern conveniences she needed. Too bad she didn't have food.

She'd been on her way to buy groceries when Brandon had interrupted her. The two bowls of bouillabaisse she'd eaten were a distant memory. Her stomach growled and she grabbed the telephone and the takeout menus she had acquired, deciding on Italian. Pizza Palace made great pizza, with plenty of melted cheese. Best of all, they delivered.

She was about to call in her order when there was a knock on her door.

"Coming," she called, hobbling to the door.

"Take your time."

At Brandon's voice she stumbled and grabbed on to the arm of the couch. Great. She nearly injured her *other* ankle. She reached the door without further incident and quickly undid the locks he'd insisted she set after he left.

He looked far too tempting holding a tray filled with several covered dishes. Dressed in the relaxed jeans he favored and a plain white T-shirt, he gave her an easy grin that had her wobbling.

"I knew you wouldn't be able to cook with that ankle, so I whipped up a little something for you."

"You didn't have to do that. I could have ordered pizza."

He shuddered and headed for the kitchen. "Pizza? When you're injured, you need comfort food. It helps with the healing process and lifts the spirits. Sit. I'll be right back."

She ignored his command and slowly followed him to the kitchen, careful to keep weight off her foot. "I'm practically healed. My ankle isn't as swollen anymore."

"You don't follow orders very well."

"Not anymore." Once she'd been the proverbial good girl, doing what her parents said. She'd trusted in their love and wisdom and followed where they led. She'd consulted them when selecting a college, relying on their input. She knew they had her best interests at heart. But for all their good intentions, they'd ended up crippling her. She'd always had them to lean on so she hadn't developed the skills necessary to recognize the wolves disguising themselves as sheep among her so-called friends.

"That can be good under certain circumstances. In others, not so much."

"Don't worry. I'll follow orders while I'm on the clock. But since we're in my apartment, it's okay to ignore you."

He laughed and pulled a stool from the breakfast bar and helped her climb on. Her skin tingled from his simple touch, something she wouldn't mind experiencing over and over again. She forced herself to ignore the sensations and make conversation. "So what did you bring?"

"Exactly what you need to ease the pain. Macaroni and cheese, my famous fried pork chops, mixed greens and, for dessert, chocolate cake."

"Will you stay and eat with me?"

He hesitated for a minute, then nodded. "I think I have enough for two."

"It looks like you have enough for four."

He set a plate in front of her, then sat down beside her. The heat from his body warmed the cold places in her heart and she yearned to move closer.

He watched her, waiting for her to eat before he did. She dipped her fork into the cheesy pasta. She closed her eyes and moaned in appreciation. "This is wonderful."

He smiled, his perfect white teeth gleaming in his brown face. The skin beside his eyes crinkled and, incredibly, he looked even more handsome than before, something she didn't believe possible. "Thanks. It's my grandfather's recipe."

She took another satisfying bite. "You should serve this in the restaurant. It would be a big hit."

"So I've been told. But it doesn't fit with the rest of the menu. I only make this for my friends."

Her heart leaped. He did consider her a friend. For a minute she'd worried that he'd brought the meal out of some misplaced sense of guilt. He'd told her they were friends, but part of her was unsure he'd meant it. She'd been used so often she'd lost her ability to trust. But, then again, Brandon had no reason to lie. He had no clue who she was, so he couldn't have an ulterior motive. At least not one that involved money. If he was after her body...well, she was after his, too.

"What's so funny?"

She didn't realize she'd laughed out loud. "I was just thinking."

"Care to share the joke?"

Not for my weight in chocolate-covered strawberries. "No joke. Your food is just as powerful as your grandfather's. Both of you bring joy. And since I can't sing I just laughed." That didn't make sense to her, but fortunately he didn't act like he thought the comment was nuts.

"The power of good food. I guarantee pizza would not have had the same result."

They ate in comfortable silence for a few minutes, enjoying the food. Finally Brandon looked at her. "Tell me about yourself."

"What do you want to know?"

He swallowed a forkful of greens before answering. "Whatever you want to share. Tell me your goals. Your dreams. Tell me about your childhood or about your family. Anything."

"Wow. There's not that much to tell. At least nothing interesting," she said, setting her fork on the edge of her plate while pondering his request. He already knew the basics of her breakup. She didn't feel the need to tell him about catching Michael-the-toad hiding cameras in his bedroom so he could make a sex video that would be his "ride to easy street." A revelation like that was definitely not in the getting-to-know-you category Brandon had in mind.

"I'm the youngest of three kids. I'm the only girl."

"How much younger?"

"I'm twenty-three. My brothers are thirty and thirty-two."

"Are you close?"

"Yes and no. They love me and I love them, but we don't hang out together. Well, they hang out but I'm generally not included." She would have loved to attend baseball games and other sporting events with them. If only they would invite her. "Our relationship is slightly better than when I was a teenager. Then they bossed me around so much it was like having two extra dads. Now they aren't as bad although they could step back some and let me live my life."

"They're protecting you."

"Spoken like a big brother."

"It's part of the unwritten code."

Arden just laughed. Somehow she knew he would see it that way.

"I can't believe they let you stay here on your own."

She punched his arm. She'd seen him in short sleeves on numerous occasions, but she was still surprised by how rock hard his muscles were. "They didn't *let* me do anything."

He raised an eyebrow. "How often do you have to call them?"

How did he know? "Every Sunday."

"That sounds about right. Still, I would expect them to pop up just to assure themselves that you're okay."

Jax and Blake in Sweet Briar? That thought chilled

her to the bone. The last thing she needed was for her brothers to show up in town. As the face of the corporation, Blake was easily recognizable. Although Jax was less visible as general counsel, he was regularly named by magazines as one of the country's most eligible bachelors. One mention that she was their sister and her vacation from real life would be over.

"Let's just change the subject."

"Sure." He topped off her lemonade. "Tell me about your dreams for the future. My grandfather always used to talk about a five-year plan. Do you have one?"

"I'm a middle school science teacher. Last year was my first year teaching."

"How'd it go?"

"Well, the kids were great."

"That's always good. I hear a *but* in there, though."

"I made the mistake of getting involved with the principal. Now I'm not sure about returning to that school in the fall. I've got some feelers out, but it might be too late to change schools next year. I might have to tough it out, which is not a pleasant thought."

"Is he the jerk you just broke up with?"

She nodded, her face growing hot with embarrassment. She couldn't believe she had been so stupid as to become involved with her boss. How clichéd.

"Do you think he'll harass you or make your life miserable? Will he make it hard for you to do your job?" Brandon's eyes were flinty as all warmth had vanished from his voice.

"No." Of that she was certain. If he tried, her brothers would grind him into dust. Even a worm like him was bright enough to know that. People might go out of their way to become friends with the Wexfords, but no one made the extra effort to become an enemy. At least not without some sort of leverage, and Michael had none. Thank goodness she'd discovered his plot before he'd had a chance to act on it.

"If he does, that would be illegal. I have a lawyer who handles restaurant business. I can contact him and see if he can refer anyone to you if you need legal assistance. It might be good to talk to someone so you can be prepared."

Arden was touched but not surprised by Brandon's offer. He was a protector by nature. Despite his claim to the contrary, he was a hero.

She put her hand atop his. A tingle danced up her fingertips and down her spine, hitting every place in between. "You know, you really are a nice guy."

"Thanks. I think."

"Why don't guys like being thought of as nice?"

"It's the way we're wired."

"It's insane."

"You're probably right." He shrugged and looked at his watch. "I had better get going." He began clearing the remains of dinner. "I'll leave the leftovers in case you get hungry later."

"Thanks." She was so full she couldn't imagine eating again, but a woman never knew when chocolate cake would call her name. She started to rise to help him, but he stopped her with a hand on her shoulder.

"You stay sitting. I'll have this clean in no time."

She knew that was true. She'd seen him clean and sanitize the much-larger kitchen at the restaurant. He had a system and worked steadily yet quickly. Sure enough, he had her kitchen in order in less time than it would take her to stack the dishwasher.

"Do you need anything before I go?" he asked as he walked to the front door. She hopped along beside him, using his arm for balance. A bunch of naughty images flitted through her mind, but she tamped them down. After he made it plain he would not kiss her again, she didn't think necking on the couch was what he meant.

"No. I'll probably just read for a while and then go to bed."

He nodded but didn't say anything more. He didn't move to open the door, and she got the feeling he wasn't any more anxious to leave than she was for him to go. The awareness that had been simmering just below the surface bubbled and boiled over. His clean masculine scent swirled around her, bringing with it memories of how good it had felt to be kissed by him.

She met his eyes and the desire in his gaze ignited a fire in her that had her skin yearning for his touch. She swayed toward him and he placed his hand on her shoulder, stilling her before she could get closer.

He heaved out a breath. "This is such a bad idea."

"Is it?"

He groaned. "Help me out, Arden."

"I can't," she whispered. "I don't have the strength."

"Hell," he muttered, pulling her close to him. He hesitated half a second as if giving her a chance to change her mind, and then lowered his mouth and kissed her. The kiss in the den had been gentle and tentative. This kiss was hot and demanding, shooting fierce need through every part of her body.

She tried to step closer to him, but he held her at a distance, not letting her get too close. Then he wrenched his mouth away from hers. "We shouldn't be doing this."

"Why? And please don't say because I work for you

occasionally." Her voice sounded breathless in her ears. Although how she heard it over the thundering of the blood racing through her veins was a mystery.

"Okay. I won't, but that won't change the fact that you do." With a finger to her lips, he once more stifled any protest she might have had. When he realized what he had done, he quickly removed his finger and shoved his hands into his pockets.

"That's not the only reason we need to keep things from getting out of control. You're coming off a bad breakup. You're vulnerable. And I'm not looking to get involved. Not now. Maybe not ever. And you may be hurt now, but I can't picture you turning your back on love forever. Let's face it, you want kids and a house. The whole nine yards. Maybe not now, but one day. I don't. There's no use starting something when we want different things."

She hated to admit it, but he was right. There was no future for them. And there never could be as long as she was keeping her identity a secret. But since he didn't want her long term, there was no reason for her to reveal who she was and ruin the paradise she'd found in Sweet Briar.

Chapter Eight

Arden awoke the next morning, bright and early. In fact, it was so early the sun had only begun to make its appearance. There was something to be said for taking an insanely long nap and then going to bed early. She had planned to read, but nothing seemed to hold her attention. After attempting to become interested in three different books, she realized she was too unsettled to focus. If she could have, she would have gone for a run. But her ankle still pained her, so she'd stayed in, taken a long bubble bath and then called Blake.

He'd been surprised to hear from her and they'd had a good conversation. Until she'd asked for money for the youth center. Then he had immediately begun to interrogate her. Where was she? How long had she been there? How could she trust these people so easily? Didn't she know people would always mention their need for money when the Wexfords were around? Hadn't she learned anything from her experiences?

She'd tried to explain that she had learned. To his credit he'd listened, something that surprised the heck out of her. But then he had always been more level-headed than Jax, which was why she'd called him. In the end Blake had agreed to keep an open mind about the Wexford Foundation making a sizable donation and he hadn't criticized her desire to make a personal one. She promised to get more information for him, which the foundation would need to make such a donation, although she had no idea how she would do that without arousing suspicion.

After that, they chatted for a few more minutes before ending the call. Perhaps it was the remnants of painkillers floating through her bloodstream, or maybe it was the good feelings from having a decent conversation with her brother, but, whatever the reason, she had slept long and deep.

Now she pointed her toes, testing her ankle. No pain. She turned her ankles in circles and didn't experience even the slightest twinge. The swelling had gone down. Standing, she walked across the room, first gingerly then with more confidence. A sigh escaped her lips. She was fine. Good, because she was hungry and the cupboard was bare. Although the diner wasn't open yet, it would be soon.

She skipped down the stairs and noticed Brandon coming across the driveway. She waved and smiled. After a hesitation so slight she wondered if she had imagined it, he lifted his hand in return.

"You're up early," she said when he was within hearing distance.

"No earlier than usual. I'm surprised to see you awake."

"No more surprised than I am. I love sleeping in, but I don't have another wink left in me. Where are you going?"

"The fish and produce markets."

"Do you want company or is this something you prefer to do on your own?"

He seemed to debate that internally. "You're more than welcome to come with me, but I have to warn you there's a lot of walking involved."

She lifted her leg and showed him her ankle. "No swelling or pain, so I'm good to go. Am I dressed okay or should I put on jeans like you?"

He looked at her and as his eyes swept over her legs, she felt the heat of his stare all the way to her bones. She knew she was blushing, but when their gazes met she didn't look away.

"Your shorts are fine. We need to get moving before all the good stuff is gone."

His voice sounded gruff, but Arden didn't let it offend her. She knew how seriously Brandon took everything that had to do with Heaven on Earth. It was his pride and joy and she was glad he was allowing her to accompany him. She found the restaurant business interesting and wanted to learn more about every facet.

Twenty-five minutes later they were walking along a pier with several small stores selling fresh fish. Trucks lined the street and the drivers raced about unloading boxes and barrels of fish and seafood. The place was jumping and Arden was immediately caught up in the energy.

"Do you come here every day?"

"Most days."

Arden rubbed her hands together. "So what exactly do you do?"

"I buy the fish and seafood that look best on a particular day and offer specials if what I buy isn't on the regular menu. It's a great way to try out new recipes and see how they go over."

"It also keeps people coming in to see what's new."

"True. Some places like the diner thrive because patrons know exactly what to expect. Their menu hasn't changed in the three years I've been here. And that works fine for them. I like having fixed menu items for people who come in for a specific dish, but I also like to create new food for the more adventurous customers. That way everyone is happy."

Arden nodded. There was a lot more to running his restaurant than met the eye. He was a shrewd businessman. Her father and brothers would be impressed. Not that they would ever meet him. She'd be back in Baltimore soon and Brandon would remain in Sweet Briar.

That thought cast shadows on her heart and dimmed the joy of the moment. But she needed to remember their relationship was only temporary and keep her heart out of it.

"Is something wrong?" Brandon's brow was drawn in concern.

"No. I'm fine."

"Are you sure? You seem a little sad."

"I'm just taking it all in. The sights. The sounds. The fresh air. Well, it's not exactly fresh, but the fish smell kind of makes me think of the ocean, which is fresh. If that makes any sense."

"It makes perfect sense. That's one of the reasons I

like coming here. Well, that and it reminds me of my grandfather."

For a moment Arden envied Brandon. He'd shared such a close relationship with his grandfather. And he had Joni and his parents and they all supported him in his endeavor. Her parents and brothers loved her, of course, but she yearned for them to see her as an adult instead of a big girl. She wanted to be respected like another adult and welcomed as a friend, not as a child to be overprotected. She knew her past behavior hadn't helped her cause, but she had changed. She just needed to show them how much.

Brandon clasped her hand and they entered one of the shops. She tightened her fingers around his, determined to enjoy the moment.

They went into several different stores where Brandon checked out the offerings. He made notes to himself on a little pad of paper he kept in his shirt pocket. By the time they were done, he'd bought an assortment of fresh fish. The shopkeepers promised to have the orders ready in two hours.

Next they drove a couple of miles to the produce market. The process was similar, with Brandon going to several stores and making notes of what he liked. He purchased a variety of fresh vegetables and fruit. Unlike the fish markets, they didn't have to wait for their purchases.

Once they'd made it through all the stalls, Brandon stacked two crates of raspberries and headed for his pickup. Arden grabbed a crate of strawberries and followed.

He turned. "Just what do you think you're doing?"

"I'm helping you. Why, what does it look like?"

"It looks like you're about to get into trouble. Now put down that heavy box."

"You're nuts," she said, placing her load in the truck beside his.

"I didn't bring you here to work."

"Then why did you bring me?"

Brandon stared into Arden's lovely eyes, temporarily lost as he tried to formulate an answer. "I brought you here to share the experience. I wanted you to enjoy it."

"I am. I'm having a great time." She wiped a hand across her forehead, leaving a red smear behind.

Before he could stop himself, he was gently brushing off the remains of the crushed fruit. Instead of removing his hand, he allowed his fingers to travel over her delicate cheekbones, down her soft cheek, finally coming to rest on her sweet lips. Pink and perfectly shaped, they called to him even without uttering a word.

"Oh, Arden," he murmured, catching her chin as he leaned forward. A small rational part of him warned that he was getting in way too deep. The bigger part of him didn't care.

He hesitated only a moment before touching his lips to hers. If she'd given even the slightest indication she didn't want him to kiss her, he would have backed off. What he saw settled it for him. In her eyes he saw a want that matched his own.

That's all he needed. He immediately closed the distance between them and captured her lips with his own. He'd planned for the kiss to be brief and gentle. But once his lips made contact with hers, he was consumed by an intense fire and all of his best intentions went up in smoke.

She stepped even closer. He inhaled her sweet scent, which added fuel to his already raging desire, and he wrapped her in his arms, holding her tight. She opened her mouth and he angled his head, deepening the kiss. He felt her heart beating against his chest, the rhythm matching the pounding of his own.

"Excuse me."

Brandon and Arden sprang apart at the sound of the amused voice. He kept his hand on her waist, though, as he looked into the grinning face of his older friend from the produce market.

"Sorry to interrupt, son. It took you so long to come back, I was afraid you forgot your blueberries and collard greens. I would hate for you to have to come all the way back here to get them." The man gestured to two smirking teens, who loaded the remaining crates into the cargo hold of Brandon's truck and then raced away.

"Thanks."

"No problem." The older man smiled as he glanced at Arden, clearly waiting for an introduction. He knew a little about Brandon's past and had been encouraging him to date. Brandon had never brought a woman with him to the markets so his friend probably assumed more than he should. Of course, he'd caught them in a serious clench, so he couldn't introduce her as his occasional employee. Well, he could, but that would embarrass and hurt Arden, something she didn't deserve.

"Ronnie, this is Arden West. Arden, this is Ronnie Leonard, owner of Leonard's Produce."

The older man extended his hand. "The freshest produce north of the equator. Come to think of it, we've got the best produce south of the equator, too."

Arden smiled and shook his hand. "It's very nice to meet you, Mr. Leonard."

"Pleasure's all mine. And it's Ronnie to all the pretty ladies."

"All right, Ronnie."

Was he flirting? Brandon frowned a little and stepped closer to Arden. Ronnie raised his eyebrows in obvious amusement.

"It's nice meeting you, Ms. West. Come see me again. I'll fix you up a box of our freshest fruit. A gift, you know."

Arden smiled at Ronnie. "I'd enjoy that. Next time I come this way I'll stop in."

"Good enough. Well, I'd better get back to the store before those kids mess up everything and I have to fire them."

Brandon laughed as the other man hurried away. But then he faced Arden, all humor gone. "We've got to stop doing this."

Arden breathed out a sigh. "I know."

"We're just friends," he said, hoping he sounded more convincing to her ears than he did to his own.

"Just friends," she repeated in a voice so soft he barely heard it. She looked over his shoulder so he couldn't read the emotions in her eyes. For some reason that bothered him more than it should have.

He was doing this as much for her as for himself. There was no sense in starting something they wouldn't be able to finish. Arden was just passing through. Neither of them was open to a relationship. She was still hurt from her last one and he wasn't willing to trust another woman.

It didn't matter that she fit so perfectly in his arms—

heck, into his life—she might have been made for him. He no longer believed such nonsense. He'd once believed that of Sylvia. What a fool he'd been. He hadn't even known her real name.

"That was fun," Arden said, finally breaking the silence as Brandon steered his truck onto the road leading to Sweet Briar.

"I'm glad you enjoyed yourself." He had to admit that he had enjoyed himself more today than he had any other time shopping at the markets. Arden had been so enthusiastic and curious, asking questions and making insightful comments so that he experienced everything anew through her eyes.

"I did." Her stomach growled loudly and she blushed prettily. "Sorry. I didn't eat yet. Do you think you could drop me off at the diner? I'll get breakfast there."

He looked at the clock. "They'll be packed right about now. How about I make something for you after we leave the stuff at the restaurant?"

"Are you sure you don't mind?"

"I haven't eaten, either. I generally eat when I get back. It's just as easy to make breakfast for two as it is for one."

"In that case, yes." She wiped at a smear on her thigh. There was another stain on her T-shirt. She pulled her shirt away from her chest and grimaced. "Do I have time to change? I won't be but a minute."

He forced his eyes away from the smooth skin of her legs and tried not to imagine what wonders were hidden under the soiled shirt. "Sure."

They dropped off the purchases at the restaurant, where his assistant chef took care of putting them into the cooler. Then Brandon drove the short distance home and parked. She hopped out, waited until he was beside her and then looked up at him. "What are we having?"

"I thought I'd throw together some crepes with fresh strawberries, a side of crispy bacon and scrambled eggs."

"You know how to make crepes?" She slapped a hand across her forehead. "Of course you know how to make crepes. Forget I said that." She aimed a thumb over her shoulder. "I'll go get changed."

He watched her go, trying not to notice the perfect curve of her hips in her denim cutoffs. Turning away from the delectable sight, he got his wayward libido under control and kept his feet moving toward the back stairs of his house and to the kitchen. As he gathered the breakfast ingredients, images of her stripping out of her clothes filled his mind. He reminded himself that they were only friends, and friends didn't see each other naked.

"How can I help?" Arden asked as she stepped into the room. She'd changed into a pair of red linen shorts and a white cotton shirt that wrapped around her tiny waist and tied beneath her perfect breasts. She'd also washed away the remnants of the strawberry from her face. She hadn't put on a bit of makeup, but she looked cover-girl beautiful. He wanted to pull her into his arms and kiss her, which despite being crazy somehow seemed right.

He yanked out a chair at the table, instead. "I've got it under control. All you have to do is have a seat and keep me company."

"Why won't you let me help? Are you afraid I'll steal your secret recipes?" Her eyes sparkled and he found himself grinning at her goofiness. She snapped her fingers. "That's it, isn't it? You're afraid I'll steal your recipe and open a crepe restaurant."

She was beautiful. Her bright smile reached the darkness in his soul, illuminating it with its warmth. Yes, her teeth were perfectly straight and incredibly white, but it was the sincerity in her expression that touched him. Too often people smiled to be polite or to cover their real emotions. He'd been guilty of that a time or two. Arden didn't do that. When she smiled it was because she truly felt joy.

"I'm not worried about you stealing my recipe. Especially since I've got it locked in here." He pointed to his head with one hand and cracked eggs into a bowl with the other. He noticed the impressed look on her face and wondered why he was showing off. He hadn't shown off for a woman in years. Not since—

He jerked his thoughts back from where they threatened to stray. He refused to let thoughts of Sylvia ruin this perfect morning. Her sudden calls out of the blue were stirring up memories he'd thought long forgotten. Clearly he couldn't keep her from calling him, but he wasn't going to let her ruin this day.

"Honestly, there's no chance anyway. I can't cook to save my life. But I make a mean microwave dinner. And toast. My toast is always the perfect shade of brown on both sides."

He laughed. "I'm not sure tossing bread into a toaster qualifies as cooking. And I know a microwave dinner doesn't come anywhere near qualifying as food."

She grinned. "You're a food snob."

"Not really. I just want my food to taste good, and

I don't want it full of chemical ingredients some mad scientist cooked up in his lab."

Despite his saying he didn't need her help, she filled the coffeepot with water and grabbed a bag of beans from the freezer. "I don't know about mad scientists, but I do admit the nuked food leaves something to be desired in the taste department."

"My point exactly." She began to set the table. Her movements were graceful, and he paused momentarily to enjoy the view before speaking again. "Food should be enjoyed. It should nourish the soul, as well as the body."

"So you believe cooking is an art."

"It's more than that. It's a labor of love. My grandfather taught me that."

She smiled at him. "Your grandfather sounds like a wonderful man."

"The best. Not a day goes by that I don't miss him. The world lost a great man when he died."

"I'm sure. But you keep him alive with everything you do. No wonder you're so particular. It's your homage to him."

Brandon nodded. She understood him in a way no one else ever had.

He whipped the first crepe onto a plate, placed it in the oven to keep warm and then quickly made another. A few minutes later, he plated the food and set it on the table. Arden poured the coffee and they sat down to breakfast.

He'd been a chef for years, and claiming he was one of the best wasn't bragging. It was the truth. He didn't indulge in false modesty. Even though he knew he'd prepared the food perfectly, he was a bit nervous as Arden lifted a bit of crepe to her mouth.

"Oh, my goodness. This is incredible." She took another bite and chewed slowly, then closed her eyes. "If people knew how good these tasted, they'd be pounding on your door demanding that you open your restaurant for breakfast."

"Then this will have to be our secret." He scooped eggs onto a fork, trying to ignore the moans that she was making.

She closed an imaginary lock on her lips. "Your secret is safe with me."

"I knew I could trust you." The words he'd spoken so easily in jest gave him pause. Did he mean them? Could he trust Arden? And if he did, did that change the kind of relationship they could have?

Chapter Nine

"Arden? This is John. I have good news for you. The part arrived last night and your car is fixed. You can pick it up anytime."

"Thanks," Arden managed to stutter before ending the call and sagging onto her bed. Her car was ready. She could leave Sweet Briar whenever she wanted. But she didn't want to leave. She was enjoying her time here, especially the time she spent with Brandon. She'd long since decided she didn't want to go to Florida, but hadn't told Brandon or Joni. After all, her car was broken down so there had been no reason to mention it. Now that it was fixed, she was going to have to tell them. Hopefully, they would let her continue to rent the garage apartment.

She was descending the stairs when Brandon pulled into the driveway. Was he coming back from the fish and vegetable markets? It was around the time they'd gotten back yesterday, so it was possible. Quashing the disappointment at not being invited to tag along and reminding herself that visiting the markets was part of his job and not a field trip, she waited until he was near enough to speak. "We've got to stop meeting this way."

He smiled, but she saw the worry in his eyes, then noticed he had his cell phone to his ear. He frowned and pushed a button, ending the call.

"Is something wrong?"

"I'm trying to reach one of my friends. He isn't answering his house or cell phones."

"Maybe he's out of town."

"No." The worry in Brandon's eyes spread to the rest of his face and his brow wrinkled. After a long moment of silence, she started to walk away. He didn't need her around while he tried to work through his problem.

She'd only taken a step when she felt his hand on her arm. The warmth of his touch sent tingles all the way to her toes in less time than it took her to exhale. This wasn't good. Brandon had been perfectly clear that he only wanted to be her friend. And given the whopper of a secret she was keeping, it was for the best. Throw in the fact that she was returning home to Baltimore, and the physical attraction was not something she needed. But how in the world could she control something that had her longing to toss away her good sense and see where another kiss would lead?

"Are you busy now?"

"Not really. Why?"

"My friend Jericho's wife died five months ago. I've been trying to get in touch with him for a couple of days. The last time I went to check on him, he said he was doing fine, but I suspect he was lying. He practically threw me off his property the minute I got there. I was thinking about taking a trip to his ranch this afternoon. Would you go with me? We can pack a lunch and ride horses. I can leave the leftovers for him."

"Are you sure about this? If he doesn't want you to visit, he definitely won't want a stranger hanging around."

"I'm sure. He may get angry with me, but he'll be polite to you. I'd get Joni to go, but she's still visiting the folks. This way I can get a look at him and leave some food so I know he'll have something to eat for the next couple of days. He won't accept the food if I just bring it to him. But if I ask to borrow some horses, he'll consider it an even trade. I know it doesn't make sense, but nothing about Jericho makes sense now."

She nodded. "You can count me in."

"Great. I'll whip up some food. We can leave in a couple of hours."

"Okay."

As Arden watched him stride away, she tried to control her pounding heart and racing imagination. She was going on a picnic with Brandon. True, she was only going because Joni wasn't around, but she'd take it. Spending time with a man who cared so deeply about his friends was a win no matter how it came about.

Brandon sealed the lid on the plastic container and set it into the wicker basket. He added ceramic plates and wineglasses, cloth napkins and silver before closing the top. Even as he worked, his mind flitted between worry about Jericho Jones and his own growing attraction to Arden. Jericho was one of the first people Brandon met when he'd moved to Sweet Briar. Jericho and his wife had been regulars at the restaurant. Brandon knew Jericho was in serious pain. Jeanette had been more than his wife. She'd been the driving force behind everything he'd done. He had turned a small ranch into a successful horse operation. Since Jeanette's untimely death, he'd lost all interest in the horses. From what Brandon could see on the rare occasions Jericho allowed him to visit, he was no longer trying to improve his business; rather, he worked sunup to sundown doing the most physical labor he could find. It was as if he wanted to work himself to death.

Brandon didn't claim to know what Jericho was going through, but Brandon knew it wasn't good for him to continue to isolate himself from his friends. From the world. Jericho had ignored Brandon's many invitations to dinner or to drop by the house or restaurant whenever he was in town. And now Jericho wasn't answering his phone. Brandon knew from personal experience that if someone didn't intervene, Jericho could spiral into serious depression. Joni and his parents had been there for him at his lowest point. He wanted to be there for Jericho.

A date with Arden provided a good excuse to drop in.

He wiped down the counters, rinsed the sponge and tossed it into the sink. After glancing around to be sure the kitchen was clean, he grabbed the basket and blanket and headed out the door. He had just placed everything in the back of his truck when Arden called out to him. Apparently, she must have been looking out her window. He smiled despite himself. Clearly she was as eager to spend time with him as he was with her.

Dressed in jeans and gym shoes and a pink-and-gray-striped shirt, she looked fresh yet sexy. Her eyes sparkled with excitement.

"I was watching for you," she said, confirming his earlier assumption. "I'm so excited to be going to the ranch. I love horses, although I haven't ridden in quite a while."

"Then let's not waste another minute." He helped her into the truck and set off down the road.

"How far away is this ranch?" Arden was peering out the window like a young girl, eagerness on her face. She turned to look at him when he didn't answer right away.

He was struck again by just how beautiful she was. Her caramel skin was perfectly clear, her eyes so open, hiding nothing. She should never play poker because her every emotion was reflected on her face. There was no way she could keep her cards a secret.

"The ranch is about ninety miles inland so it'll take us an hour or so to get there. Do you think you can contain your enthusiasm that long?"

She ran a hand over her hair. It was about an inch longer than it had been when she arrived, but it was still short and emphasized her delicate features. The style was growing on him. "If I have to. It won't be easy. My brothers always make fun of the way I get impatient. They still tease me about the time I got out of the bed in the middle of the night and slept in the car when we were going to Disney World. My parents were frantic when they woke up and I was gone. I don't think I'll ever live that down."

He caught the wistfulness in her voice. She rarely mentioned her family. Suddenly he wanted to know more about her life before she came to Sweet Briar.

"You don't talk much about your family. Why is that? Aren't you close to them?"

She shrugged and seemed to consider her response before answering. Finally she nodded. "Not in the same way that you're close with Joni. What the two of you have is pretty special."

"I know. We have another brother who we don't see as much because he's in the military. We all love each other, but I can't say that he's as good a friend as Joni."

"That's how it is with us. My brothers are close friends. They're both older than I am and still treat me like their baby sister. And to be honest, I wasn't the most mature of teens, so I might deserve it. On the plus side, I know I can always depend on them when I need them."

Brandon nodded. The van in front of them was driving too slowly, so he signaled and passed it. "Do I need to worry about your brothers coming to see me in the near future?"

She laughed and squeezed his bicep. "Don't worry. I think you can take them."

"I wasn't worried about that." He glanced over at her. "You didn't answer. Do you expect them to come and check up on you?"

"No. Why would they? I'm on a vacation."

"That's what you're calling this? A vacation?"

"Yes. It may not be what I planned, but it is definitely turning out great."

"Having your car break down and being stranded in a small town is vacation? I think I need to see your bucket list. It might need a few adjustments."

Arden laughed. "John called me today. My car is finally fixed. I'm no longer stranded, as you call it."

"So does that mean you'll be moving on?" He spoke

as casually as he could, hoping to mask the anxiety that suddenly grew inside him at the thought of her leaving so soon.

She bit her bottom lip. "Actually, I wanted to talk to you about that. I'm really enjoying my time here. Do you mind if I stay for another week or so?"

His heart thumped in his chest. She'd be in town for a while longer. He shouldn't like that as much as he did, but he couldn't help himself. He knew the relationship or whatever it was between them had an expiration date. He just wanted to enjoy her company a bit longer. At least that was the story he was telling himself. "Sure. You're welcome to stay."

"Thanks." She flashed him a blinding smile that had him doubting the wisdom of letting her remain longer. But it was too late to turn back now. And, right or wrong, part of him was glad.

"This place is beautiful," Arden exclaimed, trying to find the right words to describe the Double J ranch. So far she'd exhausted every superlative the teachers at the exclusive girls school she'd attended had drilled into her. She'd nearly run out of words and yet there was so much more to describe.

Jericho Jones, the thirtyish owner, flashed a devilish grin. The expression on his face had been grim when Brandon pulled onto his property, but he had turned on the charm when Arden hopped out of the truck. Brandon had been right about his friend's reaction. He was all smiles for her. Too bad the smile never reached his eyes, which could only be described as bleak. Her heart ached at his obvious pain. "Thanks. I'm kind of partial to this piece of land myself."

Brandon stepped closer to Arden and placed his arm around her waist, making her heart skip a beat. His hand was warm and she felt the heat through the fabric of her shirt. She immediately pictured them alone, his fingers caressing her bare skin, and a moan nearly escaped her lips.

"I was hoping we could borrow some horses," Brandon said. "Arden loves to ride. I'll show her all of the best spots. We'll be back in a couple of hours if that's okay with you."

"Sure. Take your time." Jericho's smile broadened slowly. He led the way across the brick patio, past the in-ground pool, to the stable. Arden heard horses neighing and saw a few more in the corral. "I'll saddle Buttercup for you, Arden. She's a sweet mare who'll give you a gentle ride."

Arden rubbed the sorrel's nose and was rewarded with soft nuzzling on her shoulder. "She's a pretty girl."

"That she is." Jericho moved to a large black horse. "Of course it's Diablo for you, Brandon."

"Thanks. We'll take good care of them."

"I know you will." The rancher nodded and walked away.

"You're right. He is sad," Arden said when Jericho was out of hearing range.

"Most people wouldn't pick up on it because of the way he was laughing and making jokes."

"It's so awful to see how hard he was trying to cover his pain." That was something she was familiar with. She hadn't been quite as obvious. At least she hoped not. But maybe others could see the sorrow she tried so hard to keep hidden.

"He's barely hanging on since Jeanette died in childbirth five months ago. The baby died the next day. I know that's not a long time, but I don't think he is making progress in his healing. But then, I could be wrong. The grieving process is different for everyone. I just can't help worrying."

"You're a good friend and an even better man," Arden said, meaning every word. Too bad he only wanted to be her friend. Her foolish heart wanted him to be so much more. Apparently, she didn't need as much time to recover from Michael-the-dirtbag as she thought.

Brandon seemed embarrassed by her compliment. He quickly helped her settle on her horse, then swung onto his mount with surprising ease. For someone from Chicago, a place not exactly known for its open spaces and horses, he was incredibly competent on horseback.

He led her away from the house and across a meadow. They walked until she became comfortable on her mount.

"Let's go a little faster," Arden said, increasing to a canter.

"Sure." Brandon's horse sped up eagerly. Clearly Diablo preferred a faster speed. In a few minutes they began to gallop.

"This is so much fun," Arden said, her spirits soaring. It had been quite a while since she'd felt so carefree.

Brandon nodded.

After a while, they arrived at a small lake surrounded by tall trees. Brandon dismounted and then helped Arden from her horse. She spread out her arms and turned in circles, lifting her face to the sun. The sky was perfectly blue and there wasn't a cloud for miles and miles. A gentle breeze blew, rustling the leaves in the trees, cooling her skin.

When she opened her eyes, she found Brandon staring at her, an odd expression on his face. She couldn't quite name it, but it almost looked like longing. Wistfulness. That was it. He looked wistful. Then he blinked and the expression vanished.

"I hope you're hungry," he said.

"Starved. Which is funny when you think about it. I had a huge breakfast, which would normally tide me over until lunch. But I'm really hungry when I haven't been doing much of anything. It's crazy."

"Not really. You were riding a horse."

"The horse did all the moving. All I did was sit."

"People underestimate just how much work is involved in horseback riding. You worked. You just enjoyed it."

Arden spread the blanket while Brandon unloaded the basket. He'd filled it with the most delicious-smelling food and now placed generous portions on the plates. She opened a bottle of sparkling water and poured it into two glasses, keeping one for herself and handing the other to Brandon, then accepted the plate he handed to her.

"This all looks so good."

He grinned. "Nothing but the best for you."

She lifted a small quiche to her mouth. "You're totally spoiling me."

"I'm loving every minute of it."

"Me, too." No man had ever gone to so much trouble to please her. Although this was a spur-of-the-moment date, he had taken care of every detail.

"So what do you plan to do now that your car is working?"

She sipped her sparkling water. "I'm not sure. Do you have any suggestions?"

He leaned back on his elbows, the movement drawing her attention to his muscular chest. She took another swallow in an attempt to cool down.

"Have you been to the beach yet? It's beautiful at sundown."

It probably was. And more than a little romantic. "Sounds nice. Maybe you would like to go with me some night."

He inhaled and then blew out his breath slowly. "I don't think that's a good idea."

"Why not? Don't you like beaches or sundown?"

He straightened, then reached out and touched her cheek. "You know why not. I don't want to lead you on. I'm not interested in a relationship. Not now. Not ever. I feel like we're walking a fine line now."

They were. And she was losing her balance. If she wasn't careful she would fall over the line and end up in love with him. No matter what they did, she knew it was going to hurt like heck when she left.

But she wouldn't worry about leaving now. Instead, she took another sip of her drink, determined to enjoy the wonderful meal and Brandon's company.

Chapter Ten

"So, what's going on with you and my brother?"

Arden jumped and nearly dropped the basket of folded clothes in her arms. Although the garage apartment was great, it lacked a washer and dryer. Joni had offered to let Arden use the ones in the house, but she'd refused. She didn't want to blur the lines further between tenant and landlord. Of course she'd blurred so many other lines she was beginning to think there weren't any left. Still, she felt she was doing her part to maintain order by using the machines at the Laundromat a couple of blocks away.

"You scared me."

"Sorry. I thought you saw me." Joni had just returned from her weeklong visit with her family and was wasting no time before she pounced. "Well, what's the scoop? Inquiring minds want to know."

"Inquiring minds?" Arden closed the trunk of her car and grabbed the basket off the ground. "Or is it just one mind and that would be yours?"

Joni laughed and followed Arden up the stairs and into the cozy apartment Arden had come to think of as home. "You can change things if you want. Make it your own."

"I like it just the way it is."

"I used to live here."

"You did?" Arden hung a couple of shirts on hangers and laid them across the back of a chair.

"When I first came to town. I moved here a few months after Brandon. I needed a space of my own, so he renovated it for me."

"Do you miss being on your own?"

"Nah. I like living with my brother. It's not like he tries to tell me what to do or interferes in my life. We're roommates. And we've become really good friends. Plus, he's a better cook than I'll ever be."

"That must be nice. Being friends with your brother, I mean." Arden heard the yearning in her voice.

Joni leaned forward in the chair, pouncing on that comment like a dog on a T-bone steak. "You and your brother don't get along?"

"Brothers. I have two. And it's not that. They're best friends and I'm sorta out there."

"Don't give up hope. Brandon and I weren't always close." Joni twirled her hair around her fingers. "But the real question is, how close are you and my brother?"

"Back to that, are we?"

"Yes. Notice how smoothly I transitioned."

Arden laughed.

"So come on, friend, spill."

Such a simple word. *Friend.* And yet it meant so

much. A friend was someone to share good times and bad. Someone to laugh with about a guy she liked. And knowing that Joni included her in that category was great.

"There's nothing to spill. We're friends." The word didn't make her as happy when she thought about it in relation to Brandon. But he'd emphasized that they were just friends after they'd shared kisses so hot her lips were singed. Message received.

"Really? What about him carrying you up the stairs? That sounds like something serious and totally out of character for Brandon."

"Who told you that? Certainly not Brandon."

"Girl, please. Getting information out of him is harder than prying open clams with your fingernails."

That was a relief. After having a so-called boyfriend who was going to share the most intimate details of her life with the entire internet if she hadn't caught him first, it was nice to know that Brandon respected her privacy.

"Then how did you know? You weren't even in town that day. And how was Chicago, by the way?"

"Chicago was just as I'd left it. As to your other question, I have my ways."

Arden put her hands on her hips and waited.

"Okay. Kristina Harrison saw you. You remember, the owner of the Sunrise."

Arden nodded.

"She stopped by to talk to Brandon and saw him carrying you up the stairs. According to her, it was quite romantic."

It had been. But Arden would never admit that, even to herself. Especially to herself. She had walls around her heart for a reason. Brandon was chopping away at them even if he didn't know it. "I twisted my ankle and he helped me inside. That's all."

"Rats. That's just what he said."

"Sorry to disappoint you."

"So there was no kissing."

Arden's face heated and she didn't answer. She didn't want to lie, but she didn't think Brandon would appreciate her discussing the specifics of their relationship with his sister.

"So you did. I knew it."

"Surely you don't want details."

"About my brother? No way. That's just icky. Of course, it would be good to have something to taunt him with. You know, as payback for all those times he teased me when we were kids. But, seriously, I'm just happy that he's finally moving on."

"He's not moving on. At least not with me. It was just a friendly kiss between pals." A kiss so hot her lips were still sizzling. But that was a result of chemistry. Even she knew better than to confuse physical attraction with something deeper.

Joni didn't look convinced, but thankfully she let the subject drop. "What are you doing for dinner tonight? I know you're not helping Brandon since he has hired a couple of new waitresses and you're not covering as many shifts."

"I actually haven't thought about it."

"Come to girls' night out with me."

"What's involved?"

"It's nothing formal. My friends and I get together whenever we can. Sometimes we go to a movie or dinner. Tonight we're meeting at Kayla's house. She's married to John, the mechanic who fixed your car. He's grilling and the rest of us are bringing sides."

"I thought you said it was girls' night," Arden said.

"John's not hanging around. He's going out with the guys from the choir."

"He sings?" Arden choked out. John sounded like a foghorn, but maybe the church was desperate. Small towns would have a smaller talent pool.

"Goodness, no. He's terrible. He plays the drums. Anyway, we're going to have a great time. We'll eat, then just hang around and talk. It's a lot of fun and a great chance for you to meet more people."

"You sure they won't mind?"

"Positive. In case you haven't noticed, we're a welcoming bunch in Sweet Briar."

She had noticed that everyone smiled and said hello when they passed her on the street. The other people at the Laundromat talked to her while they washed their clothes. She'd had conversations with the waitresses at the restaurant. Everyone had been nice. But Joni was taking it a step further by including Arden in her intimate group of friends.

"In that case, I'd love to come. Should I bring anything?"

"That's not necessary. You're my guest."

Arden grinned. "I can hardly wait."

At six o'clock Arden jumped into Joni's car and they were off. After a short and scenic drive through town, Joni parked in front of a redbrick house with a well-groomed yard. Instead of heading for the front porch, Joni and Arden followed the sound of feminine laughter around the side of the house and to the backyard.

Several women lounged in chairs grouped around the patio while John manned the grill.

Dressed in jeans and a Carolina Panthers jersey, he looked like he was having the time of his life. He took foil packets off the grill and set them on a platter. "These vegetables and chicken are nice, but are you sure you don't want some meat? I have some great steak that will put a little meat on your bones."

"Our bones are happy with the meat they have," one of the women said, tossing a napkin at him.

He shrugged and flashed a grin. "Don't say I didn't offer." Done with the grill, he went to a petite woman and kissed her long and deep before waving goodbye.

"Everyone, this is Arden," Joni said, sweeping her into the middle of the women. "She's staying with Brandon and me for a while."

"Hi," she said, suddenly ridiculously nervous.

"I'm Kayla. We haven't officially met yet although I've seen you around. Welcome to my home. That was my husband who just left." She pointed to each of the women, introducing them by name. "That's Liz, and Hannah, and Katrina, and Veronica." They each waved back in turn. "Help yourself to a drink and come sit down. We want to know all about you."

Arden grabbed a can of soda and joined the group. "I'm afraid you'll be bored to tears."

"Kayla, a little bird told me you had news," Joni said.

"Yeah. There are no secrets in this town. I'm pregnant again."

"That's wonderful," Liz said, hugging their hostess. Arden added her congratulations to those being offered by the other women.

"I'm happy, although I could strangle my husband. I seem to get pregnant whenever he looks at me."

"You must not have paid enough attention in biology. It's not the looks that get you into trouble. It's what happens afterward," Joni quipped.

Everyone laughed, including Kayla. When everyone quieted, she turned to look at Arden. "So how do you like our town?"

Arden looked at the eager faces of the women. They actually seemed interested in her answer. Maybe they were just being polite, but she didn't get that vibe. If they were Joni's friends, they were probably as nice as she was. That thought set her at ease and she knew she could enjoy herself. "I like it. Sweet Briar is beautiful. The people are great."

"And the men are so good-looking," Veronica added. "Especially a certain chef of a fabulous restaurant."

Joni made the time-out sign with her hands. "No talking about my brother. That's just too weird."

"Okay. Then I won't mention his cute butt," Hannah added.

"Or that muscled chest," Liz put in, fanning her face with a napkin.

"Ignore them. They just do this because it bugs me." Joni shook her unopened can of cola and aimed it at the other women.

"Okay. We give. Let's talk about you and the mayor."

Joni rolled her eyes. "I told you, move along. There's nothing to see there. Lex and I are just friends."

"I don't understand you," Hannah said, a sudden frown marring her face. She wagged a manicured finger in Joni's direction. "That man is hot."

"Seriously hot," Veronica added. "Ice cubes melt the minute he walks into a room."

Arden did agree that the mayor was attractive in a pretty-boy way. She just didn't feel the same pull she felt with Brandon. Brandon may not have been as classically handsome as Lex, but something about him lit her fire.

"I'm not disputing his hotness," Joni said. "I do have eyes in my head. I'm just not interested in a romance with him or anyone else right now."

"Are you crazy?" Hannah gaped, then shook her head again. She began to list his good qualities, using her fingers to count. "He's hot. He's nice. He treats you well. You know he went out on a limb to convince the city council to give the youth center that funding."

"And don't forget the best quality of all," Liz said.

"What's that?" Arden asked, getting into the spirit. Listening to the other women, she wondered if Joni should consider having a relationship with the mayor. She'd seen them together and sparks did fly. The pull between them was so strong you could practically see it. Evidently, he had even more good qualities than she knew.

"He's rich."

Arden nearly choked on her drink. "What?"

"He's loaded. His entire family is."

"That doesn't matter to me," Joni said.

"Really? My mama always said it's just as easy to love a rich man as it is to love a poor one." Liz laughed.

"Easier," Hannah chimed in. "You don't have the financial worries that other couples do."

Arden knew they were joking, but jokes often contained insights into a person's true feelings. Maybe these women did believe wealth was a good enough reason to become involved with someone. But then they laughed. And they had listed many of Lex's other qualities first. Maybe she was overreacting. She was still raw from having been involved with someone who actually lived by those words. Of course Michael-the-worm hadn't loved her, but he'd certainly been willing to fake it in order to get his hands on her trust fund. She forced that thought away. She refused to let thoughts of him ruin another of her days. That fool was in the past and that was where he was going to stay.

The evening passed quickly and plans were made to get together again the following week at Hannah's house. If the weather was good, they'd swim in her pool. Arden exchanged numbers and even made lunch plans with Veronica for the following week.

"Did you have a good time?" Joni asked after they said goodbye to everyone and headed to the car.

"The best. Everyone was great." Arden fastened her seat belt and leaned back, the pleasure of the evening still bubbling inside her. Aside from the one little hiccup when the subject of marrying for money had come up, everything had been wonderful. "Thanks for including me. I feel like I've just made a bunch of really great friends."

Joni pulled away from the curb and blew the horn, tossing a final wave to Kayla, who stood on her front lawn. "That's because you did make a bunch of really great friends. Before you know it, you won't be able to remember living anywhere but here. You'll put down roots so deep and so fast your head will spin."

Joni's words struck a chord. She could easily see the picture Joni painted. And, boy, did she like it. But she knew she would never be able to remain here. The day was rapidly approaching when she'd have to give up the identity of Arden West, waitress, and return to her life as Arden Wexford, heiress.

Chapter Eleven

Arden and Joni were blocks away from Heaven on Earth when Joni's phone rang. She put it on hands-free and answered.

"Is this my favorite sister in the world?"

Arden's heart sped up as Brandon's voice filled the car. It was as if he'd suddenly materialized beside her. She smiled and glanced at Joni, who looked back at her with a raised eyebrow. Arden tried to hide her expression, but when Joni smirked she knew it was too late.

"Nope. She's home in bed because she has to be at the youth center early tomorrow."

"Come on, Joni. I wouldn't call you unless it was an emergency. Lydia went home sick. I only need you for a couple of hours."

Arden looked at her tired friend and spoke up. "I can come. We're not far away."

She heard him expel his breath. What was that about? Finally he replied. "Thanks. I owe you."

"I'm not keeping score."

Joni disconnected the call and turned to Arden. "I'm not going to ask what's going on between you two. That's none of my business. But I will ask you to be careful with my brother's heart. He's been hurt. It changed him. He was the most playful and charming guy. Now he tries to protect himself."

"As are you."

"I'm his sister."

"I would never hurt Brandon. At least not on purpose."

"Good enough." Joni smiled and pulled to the curb. "Thanks for helping my brother."

"I'm just returning one of many favors."

"I thought you weren't keeping score."

Arden laughed and ran inside the building. Ten minutes later she was dressed in the uniform Joni kept at the restaurant for emergencies. Every seat in the dining room was filled. After she found out which tables she would be serving, she went to each one, introduced herself and asked what the patrons needed. She delivered the requested items with a smile, easing into the familiar routine.

The night flew quickly and before long the last customers—a party of eight—left amid boisterous laughter. The waitresses followed soon after, followed by the kitchen staff. As had been her practice whenever she worked, Arden helped Matt clean. When the dining room was straightened, she let him out, locked the door and then joined Brandon in the kitchen.

He looked up from a counter he was wiping. "Thanks. You really saved me tonight."

"No worries." She looked around the sparkling kitchen. It looked clean, but you never knew. Brandon was a stickler, and what looked perfect to her might not be perfect to him. "You need any help?"

He shook his head. "I'm finished." He disposed of the cloth and then gestured for her to proceed out the kitchen. He flipped off the lights, then followed her. He grabbed the linens, turned on the alarm, then led her to his truck.

"How was girls' night out?" he asked as they drove down the silent streets. The night was dark and peaceful. Sweet air blew through the open windows. It was as if they were the only two people in the world.

"It was fun. Everybody was so nice."

"Why do you sound surprised?"

She couldn't explain about her past experiences without going into detail about who she was. But maybe it was time for her to do just that. She'd been around Brandon long enough to know he wasn't the type to let a large bank account change his behavior. His character was solid. He wasn't greedy and there wasn't a deceitful bone in his body. She was ashamed that she'd ever thought he could be. Her only excuse was that past hurts had made her cautious and suspicious.

"I've had some pretty bad experiences that have made me more jaded than the average person my age."

He nodded as he pulled to the curb, but his attention was clearly not on what she was saying. She followed his gaze to his front porch. The light was on, illuminating a woman sitting on the front steps. Joni was standing beside her with her arms crossed. Even from this distance, it was clear from Joni's rigid posture that she was fuming.

"Son of a..." Brandon slammed the brakes and

jumped from the vehicle, leaving the keys dangling in the ignition. Arden felt uncertainty battling with a willingness to help, as well as plain old curiosity. She removed the keys, locked the doors and slowly walked to the porch.

"I tried to get her to leave, but she refuses. I'm tempted to call the police. Really, I'd like to drag her off by her hair."

"It's okay, Joni. Go inside. I'll take care of her once and for all." He never took his eyes off the other woman.

"What about Arden?"

Brandon blinked and looked around. He'd been so focused on the other woman that he had forgotten all about her. "Thanks for your help. I'll talk to you later."

She nodded, clearly dismissed. She handed him his car keys. "Sure. I was glad to help." She started around to the side of the house toward the garage, questions bombarding her from every direction. Who was that woman? What did she have to do with Brandon? It was obvious he was angry with her, but was that anger simply love turned inside out? Was she the woman who had hurt Brandon?

If so, did she want him back?

Would he take her back?

Brandon inhaled deeply, trying to gain control of his emotions as he stared at the woman he'd hoped never to see again. Sylvia. He couldn't believe she was here. He'd been clear that he didn't want her in his life. He'd told her as much. And then he had not answered another of her calls. Even she should have figured out that the last thing he wanted was for her to show up at his front door.

Did she think she would have an advantage if she

blindsided him? Not a chance. Maybe if he was still in love with her, but those tender feelings had died the night he almost did.

He looked around. Although Arden had left, Joni still stood on the porch, her body shaking with barely contained fury. Sylvia must have sensed the danger, because her eyes kept darting to Joni. Sylvia looked ready to take flight at any moment.

"I've got this, Joni. Go on to bed." He looked over at Sylvia and didn't try to mask his distaste. Joni still didn't move so he repeated himself. "I'll handle this and be inside in a minute."

"Okay." His sister glared at Sylvia, then stalked inside.

When the door was firmly closed behind Joni, Brandon turned his attention to Sylvia. "What part of leave me the hell alone is too difficult for you to understand?"

He expected her to become defensive or, worse yet, to turn on the sex appeal. She'd had that act down in spades. Tall and curvy, she'd known how to dress to accentuate her attributes and attract a man. He'd fallen into her trap even as she was using him to get close to Jason Smith, the silent partner in the restaurant where Brandon had worked in Chicago. Nothing about her had revealed that she was a rogue FBI agent seeking revenge on the man she'd blamed for her brother's death even if it had meant pretending to be in love with Brandon and endangering his life.

He stared at her. He'd never seen her look anything other than well put together. Even when she was pulling a gun and shooting at drug lords, she'd been wearing designer clothes. The porch light wasn't as good as daylight, but he could see her clearly. Her previously long, thick hair looked thin and dull, her clothes cheap. She had definitely come down in the world.

She dug short, unpolished nails into the palms of her hands. "I understand. I don't want to make trouble. I just needed to see you."

"Well, now you've seen me. You can go."

He started to walk around her and she grabbed his forearm. He wanted to shove her away, but a lifetime of being taught never to hurt a woman wouldn't let him. He settled for lifting her hand away and stepping back.

"Please. Just listen to me. I promise to never bother you again."

"I can accomplish the same thing with a restraining order."

"Please, Brandon. For old times' sake."

That was the wrong thing to say. "You are mistaken if you think bringing up the past is a way to win points with me."

"I'm sorry. You're right. But please…" She looked more uneasy than he'd ever seen her.

He paused, still glaring at her.

She took a deep breath. "I'm here to make amends."

"What?"

"I want to make amends."

"You have got to be kidding me. What sort of angle are you working now? Don't tell me—you're investigating someone in town and need me as part of your new cover."

She flinched but didn't argue back. "No angle. You are one of the people I hurt. I want to apologize to you and try to make it right."

He looked at her again. *Really* looked. Her appearance wasn't the only thing that had changed. Her demeanor was different. Less confident. Humble. Unsure. He leaned his head back and looked at the sky and then blew out a long breath. She might actually be sincere. And even if she wasn't, she was determined to speak her piece. He was willing to give her a chance if that meant he'd be rid of her for good. "You have five minutes."

She nodded and rubbed her hands against her slacks, then hesitated as if she didn't know where to start.

He didn't say a word. He certainly wasn't going to help her get started. She'd been bugging him for weeks. She should have scribbled notes on cards. Leaning against the porch post, he crossed his arms and waited. She only had five minutes. Whether she talked or not was up to her. But when her time was up, he was gone.

"I loved my brother. Evan was the cutest baby and the best kid in the world. When he turned thirteen he changed. My parents adored him and didn't see the change until it was too late."

She stared into the distance, then looked at Brandon. He didn't want to get sucked into her story and start to feel compassion for her, so he tapped a finger on his watch.

"Right. Well, Evan started getting into trouble with the police when he was sixteen. I'd already begun working for the FBI. I thought it would help if he came to stay with me in Chicago for the summer so I could keep an eye on him. I even had a job lined up for him." She shook her head slowly. Sorrowfully. "Bringing Evan to Chicago was a mistake. Within a week he'd found a group of messed-up kids to hang around. I didn't know it, but he had started selling drugs. He got on the wrong side of Jason Smith, a major dealer who just happened to be a silent partner in the restaurant where you worked. He had Evan killed.

"My parents blamed me. They said their son would still be alive if I hadn't convinced them to let him come to Chicago. Maybe they were right." Her voice broke and she wiped a tear from beneath her eye. "I was blinded by pain. That's no excuse, I know, but I couldn't let Smith get away with murdering my brother. I needed a way to get close to him and you were it. I'm sorry."

Despite his intent to keep his heart hard toward her, a part of Brandon understood. He would lose it if something happened to Joni. "Are things better with your family?"

She shook her head. "I convinced myself that if I got justice—really revenge—for Evan's death they would forgive me. I was wrong. I went to see them after…after. They told me I wasn't welcome at their home anymore. As far as they were concerned, I died to them the same day Evan did."

"Oh. Wow." He couldn't imagine parents being so cold to their own child. Families were supposed to pull together in times of tragedy, not turn on their own.

"I was already in trouble at work and their rejection tipped me over the edge. I went off the rails. I stopped caring about myself and started drinking. I hit rock bottom about a year ago and stayed down there for a while. I lost my job. My condo. The few friends I had left. Anyway, about a month ago I started a program. Got a job. Started to make amends to the people I hurt.

"I know you want me out of your life, and I'll stay away. I just wanted to explain what happened and to apologize. I am so sorry you got hurt. I did care about you. I just cared about revenge more."

He nodded. Who was to say he wouldn't have acted the same way in her situation? Blind pain could bring out the worst in even the best person. "I forgive you."

Her eyes met his and something akin to hope flashed there. "Thank you. You have no idea how much that means to me."

He extended a hand. He hadn't known what had motivated her to act as she had. Now that he did, he could understand. "I wish you the best in the future."

"Thanks. I hope the same for you."

Brandon watched her drive away. Miraculously, he felt lighter than he had in years. Forgiving Sylvia had lifted the distrust he'd held inside for so long. He didn't need the walls around his heart any longer. He was finally free to love again.

Chapter Twelve

Arden heard the knock on her door. She'd been anticipating it since she'd walked away from Brandon an hour ago. While she'd waited, she'd showered and changed into a tank and shorts, then polished her toenails a cheery red.

"Coming," she called as she removed the last cotton ball from between her toes. She scooped up the others and shoved them into her pocket. She'd dispose of them later.

"I'm glad you're still up," Brandon said, walking into the room. "I imagine you have quite a few questions."

"I know your private life is none of my business, but…" She shrugged and her words faded out as she didn't quite know how to continue. She had felt those full warm lips on hers on several occasions. Been wrapped in his strong arms. She and Brandon had been spending a lot of time together. Nothing official had been said, but their relationship was evolving into something more than friendship. At least it felt that way to her. She wanted to know more about the mystery woman and her relationship with Brandon.

"Can we sit down?"

Arden nodded and joined him on the small love seat. She had been around him for a while, but it still amazed her how completely he overwhelmed a room. The space suddenly felt a lot smaller. More intimate. And, darn it, despite the fact that there was a lot to be straightened out between them, when the heat from his body reached her, her stomach did a little topsy-turvy thing and she longed to lean into him and let his warmth envelop her. She settled for leaning against the armrest and facing him.

"Sylvia is my ex-fiancée."

The warmth vanished and was immediately replaced by a chill. "Fiancée?"

"*Ex*-fiancée. Sort of."

"You're not making sense." At least she didn't think he was. It was hard to be sure when the word *fiancée* kept reverberating in her mind, crashing into the other words he was saying.

"I told you that I used to work in a restaurant in Chicago." He glanced at her. She managed to nod. "I didn't know it at the time, but one of the partners was actually a drug dealer. I'm talking big-time. He didn't have any input in the daily operation of the business, so we didn't have any interactions to speak of.

"One day, Sylvia came to the restaurant. I was making the rounds, talking with some customers. She introduced herself. I thought she was attractive, but that was about it. A few days later she returned and later became a regular. We struck up a friendship and eventually started dating. It wasn't unusual for her to stop in after work and then hang out until closing time." He shook his head and Arden wondered what he was thinking. Was he remembering the good times he'd shared with this other woman? His face certainly didn't give anything away.

"Anyhow, eventually I proposed and she said yes."

A lump formed in Arden's stomach. She wanted to know more, but at the same time she wanted to cover her ears and hum show tunes loudly. He must not have noticed her inner turmoil because he kept right on talking.

"A few months later we were at the restaurant. It had just closed for the day. We were walking to her car when all hell broke loose. One minute the night was quiet and the next bullets were flying. Sylvia was right in the middle of it. A guy was shooting at her. I knocked her down to protect her. The next thing I knew I was waking up in the hospital. I'd been shot three times."

"What?" Arden thought she was prepared for anything, but hearing about a gun battle when she expected to hear about an unfaithful fiancée was something no one could prepare for.

"It turns out Sylvia was an FBI agent. Her brother had been murdered by a drug dealer and she wanted revenge. The restaurant's silent partner was that drug dealer. She'd been hanging around so she could find out how he operated. A takedown had been planned for that night, but a police officer was on Smith's payroll and alerted him to the plan before it went down."

"Wow. Just…wow."

"That's one way of putting it, although I've used more colorful words myself."

"I bet. When did this happen? And why is she here now? Don't tell me she wants to get back together with

you." *Please, no.* But then Arden would soon be returning to Baltimore, so what did it matter? Still, it felt like
someone had shoved a knife into her stomach and started
twisting it.

"Just over three years ago. I moved to Sweet Briar when
I was well enough. Sylvia said she came here to make
amends."

"Did she even love you?" What would be the worse
answer? Hearing that she did and sacrificed that love,
or hearing that she didn't and had only been using him?

"Who knows. She said she did, but how can I ever
be sure? She lied about everything else, including her
name. One part of me understands why she did that. She
was undercover, after all. But, still, she created a whole
different identity. I don't think I ever knew who she
was inside. At this point, I don't think it even matters."

"Brandon, I'm sorry that happened to you." Arden's
voice was reduced to a whisper. She tried to swallow
but her mouth had gone dry.

"Hell, it's in the past, but I know you have an active imagination and I didn't want to leave you in here
imagining the worst. I wanted you to know the truth."
He stood and stretched. "I'm beat and I guess you probably are, too. I'd better let you get some sleep."

She nodded and tried to stay calm as fear gripped
her heart. Why hadn't she told him the truth sooner? He
might not be willing to listen to her explanation about
why she'd used an alias all this time. And didn't that stink.

Maybe she should just leave town without telling
him who she really was. Her car was running and she
could leave anytime. Would she? That was the question
she couldn't answer.

* * *

After a restless night of tossing and turning, Arden hadn't reached a decision on whether to leave or stay. She did know that she was going to come clean with Brandon and Joni. She didn't feel comfortable continuing to keep her identity a secret when she knew the hurt Brandon had experienced at the hands of another woman who'd deceived him. Actually, she had begun to feel uncomfortable before then. She wished she had acted sooner.

Oddly enough, unless someone referred to her as Arden West, she hadn't thought about the name she was using. She simply thought of herself as Arden. Now that she knew the type of person Brandon was, she knew he would have treated her with the same kindness whether or not he'd known her real last name. Of course, hindsight was twenty-twenty.

She did know one thing for sure: she was through running from difficult situations. She was going to face her problems head-on. That was what she should have done with Michael-the-pond-scum. When she'd overheard him plotting to secretly make a sex tape so he could blackmail her, she should have confronted him. Instead, she'd tucked her tail between her legs and left town like she'd been the weasel. She'd run when she should have stood and fought. After all, she had recorded him plotting on her cell phone. She didn't have everything he'd said, but she had enough to prove what he had been planning. Her brothers wouldn't have acted like cowards. They would have let that jerk know he'd made the mistake of his life when he decided to take on a Wexford. They would have fought as hard and dirty as necessary. And they would have won.

Maybe part of her problem was that she had relied on Jax and Blake to fight her battles for her. Standing on her own two feet meant doing it herself instead of running away. Depending on herself actually meant being dependable. She would start today. Now. She had to act no matter how afraid she was of losing Brandon.

That decided, she dressed quickly, combed her hair and headed down the stairs. She'd expected Brandon's truck to be gone, but still felt a twinge of disappointment that he wasn't around now when she was feeling strong. Who knew if she would be this ready to confess her wrongdoing in an hour or two?

"Hey, Joni," Arden said, crossing the back lawn to where her friend stood hanging laundry to dry in the sun and fresh air. She was tempted to confide the truth about her identity to Joni as sort of a practice run, but didn't. She had to tell Brandon first. Sure, she was close to Joni, but she had begun to feel a different type of closeness with Brandon since the first time he'd pressed his tantalizing lips to hers. As she'd listened to him describe his relationship with his former fiancée—man, she hated the sound of that—she could tell he still carried the pain of betrayal. And if she didn't do something immediately, she would be the one hurting him. Her stomach churned at the thought.

"You're up mighty early."

"I know. It's becoming a habit. I haven't decided whether it's good or bad. You're up pretty early yourself."

"I have so much to do I have to get up at this ungodly hour just to keep my head above water. The summer days are really hectic at the youth center. It's as if kids save up all of their energy throughout the school year and explode over the summer. We have so many fun things to do and they're determined to do them all at least once." Joni reached into a clothes basket and grabbed a wet pillowcase, draped it on the clothesline and pinned it in place. "I'm going to be working like a madwoman these next few days, so I want to reward myself by sleeping on sun-dried sheets when I finally get to fall into bed."

"Need help?"

"With the laundry or the youth center?"

"Either. Both." Being busy might help her settle her nerves and hold on to her resolve to come clean with Brandon.

"Yes to both."

Arden pulled out another pillowcase and secured it to the line. "I love the smell of clothes dried by the sun."

"Me, too. I try to dry my laundry this way as often as possible, but normally I'm so busy I just toss everything in the dryer."

"What kind of help do you need at the youth center?"

"We're about to have our summer bash."

"What's that?"

Joni rolled her eyes. "Organized insanity."

Arden laughed and helped Joni hang a queen-size sheet. She wondered idly if it belonged to Brandon and imagined lying on his bed with him before forcing herself to pay attention to what Joni was saying.

"Seriously, it's a weekend-long festival. The whole town is involved." Joni hung the last bit of laundry on the line and dropped a couple of unused clothespins into the basket. "The summer bash is like the rest of the summer on steroids. We have activities day and night and a giant sleepover. We start Saturday at noon with a parade through town. We don't have many floats, but kids ride their bikes or pull wagons. The high school marching band comes. We even have a fire engine, which delights the younger set. Fingers crossed the weather is great because we'll be at the beach a lot of the weekend. We end things with fireworks. Then I'll come home and collapse."

"Sounds hectic and wonderful. What can I do to help? And when?"

"I could use you any time you can help out."

"Done."

"Would you be interested in judging a talent show Saturday after dinner?"

"You mean with singing and dancing? Sure. Sounds fun."

"It is. The hardest part is finding unbiased judges. Most everyone in this town is related to one of the contestants. I had one mother who didn't believe anyone was more talented than her little Tommy who fell off his pogo stick every other hop. She and another judge whose daughters perform synchronized hula-hooping nearly came to blows. True story. Made me think we should add mud-wrestling moms. Of course, if you would rather participate in the show, you can do that, too."

"Adults participate?"

"Yep. It's a hoot although they can't win any of the prizes. You wouldn't believe some of the talent we have in this town."

"I think I'll stick to judging. I wouldn't want to embarrass myself."

"Good enough. If you can be at the center around noon today we can get set up. The weekend will be here before you know it and there's a lot of work to be done before then."

"Okay." Arden wandered away, wondering why she was getting more involved with the community instead of distancing herself before the truth about her identity came out. Of course, helping at the youth center gave her one more reason to stay in town longer. Truthfully, she saw the value in the work Joni did and she wanted to be an active participant. Anybody could donate money—and she still planned to do that—but Joni needed willing workers. She was making a difference in the lives of so many people. By helping, Arden was making a difference, too.

And there was always the hope that Brandon would understand why she had lied and forgive her. If that happened, everything would be good. Somehow she didn't think it was going to be that easy. She didn't have to be a fortune-teller to predict that messy days were in her near future. But she would wait until after the festival was over before telling Brandon the truth. She wanted to help at the center and didn't want to risk bad feelings on his or Joni's part. What difference would a couple of days make?

"I've never been so happy to see the end of the night," Arden said, slipping her feet from her gym shoes without bothering to untie them, dropping onto a plush sofa in Joni's office and stretching out. Brandon raised his eyebrows at the way she had appropriated the entire couch, but she didn't move. It was three o'clock in the morning and she was beat, so it was every man for himself. "I could sleep standing up."

The summer bash was even more insane than Joni

had warned her. Kids must have come from all over the state to participate. Arden was glad that she was around to volunteer. Joni had definitely needed her help. And she was equally as glad that another volunteer had relieved her minutes ago.

"Don't tell me a few kids wore you out," Brandon said as he closed the door behind them. The scent of chlorine from the center's swimming pool clung to his hair. He pulled the chair from behind the desk, then sat across from her. The tweens and teens were scattered throughout the center participating in various activities while the little ones were sleeping off a sugar high. At least they were supposed to be sleeping.

"They aren't kids. Kids don't move that much." She ran a hand through her damp curls. She wouldn't be surprised to discover strands of gray throughout the black in the morning. "They're motion machines. They're like that carnival game."

"Which one?"

"You know. The one where the furry little animal sticks his head out of a hole. You try to hit him, but it's too late. He's popping out another hole. You can never catch him."

"Whac-A-Mole."

"Exactly. As soon as I got one kid settled down another kid popped up. It's some kind of plot, I tell you. Kids against the adults. They're trying to run us ragged so they can take over the world. Or at least Sweet Briar."

Brandon leaned back and stretched his long legs in front of him, looking completely relaxed. How could he look like he could go on a three-mile run right now when Arden couldn't move a muscle to save her life? But, he wasn't weighed down by a guilty secret that was beginning to make breathing difficult. Her conscience was becoming like Whac-A-Mole. Every time she felt justified in keeping her secret, guilt popped free and stared her in the face.

Brandon's deep laughter had her pushing that guilt down with even more determination. She was going to tell him the truth. So why not enjoy the moment? Besides, she didn't think she'd ever seen him this carefree and lighthearted. Telling him the truth now might ease her sense of guilt, but it would ruin his pleasure. After everything he'd endured, he deserved some plain old fun.

"Arden, don't take this personally, but you're nuts."

"Don't laugh. I saw the mayor here earlier. He was helping Joni with a bunch of kids. I haven't seen him since then. They've probably tied him up somewhere and gagged him so he can't call for help. Something sinister is definitely happening here."

Brandon finally stopped laughing enough to speak. "I don't think it's a plot by kids to take over the world. It's the abundance of sugar. I warned Joni that she should insist on fruit and vegetables as snacks, but she wouldn't listen. She let parents bring all kinds of cookies and candy. Now the kids are overdosing on sugar and you're paying for it."

Arden covered a yawn. Who would have thought spending the day supervising a handful of seven- and eight-year-olds would be more tiring than working a busy shift at the Heaven on Earth? "How were things at the restaurant tonight?"

"Good. We were full all night."

No surprise there. The dining room was usually filled to capacity and Brandon had mentioned expanding into the building next door if the numbers worked. "How did your new special go over?"

Brandon smiled and heat bloomed in her stomach, pushing aside guilt in a way that her mind hadn't been able to. Arden couldn't help being attracted to him. He was so handsome, although his looks were only a small part of his appeal. He had such a kind heart. After working in the restaurant, he had come to the youth center to help his sister with the kids. He had to be exhausted, but that hadn't stopped him from hopping into the pool and playing water volleyball with some of the high school kids. She'd been hustling the younger kids out of the shallow end after their swim, but she'd managed to sneak an occasional peek at his bare torso. The water dripping from his hair and trickling down his muscular chest had warmed her despite the fact that she'd been waist deep in cold water.

"I'm pleased to say it was a hit."

"I'm not surprised. I loved it."

"Thanks. Your support means a lot to me."

He sounded so sincere Arden felt herself blushing.

He rose, lifted her feet from the sofa, sat down and placed her feet on his lap. Before she could guess his intentions, he began to massage her right foot. A satisfied moan slipped from her lips. No man had ever treated her with such care.

"I take it you like that?" His voice was deeper than ever and it sent shivers down her spine. His hands were gentle yet firm as they soothed the ache in that foot, then switched to her left.

She sighed and closed her eyes. "More than words can express."

"Then don't try to use words." His hands worked

their magic as he increased the pressure on the balls of her feet, drawing murmurs of satisfaction from her lips. Surely it couldn't be wrong to enjoy this moment. And maybe a few more.

The silence of the room surrounded them, wrapping them in an intimate cocoon. It was as if they were the only people in the world. A single lamp offered soft illumination while a line of moonlight filtered through an opening in the otherwise closed curtains. Brandon leaned closer and Arden's senses were filled with the scent of clean male with that hint of chlorine. His fingers moved over her feet, traveling to her ankles and calves. His hands moved gently over her legs, leaving tingling heat with each touch.

Brandon made an agonized sound and stopped caressing her. "I know I should keep my distance, but I just can't keep from wanting to touch you."

Arden opened her eyes and took in Brandon's tortured expression. Sitting up, she reached a hand to his cheek. "What if I want you to touch me?"

"Arden." His voice issued a warning she chose to ignore. "I know you've been hurt. I don't want to add to that. I'm still working out some things."

Which just proved how nice a guy he was. And since he was so nice, so caring, he would understand why she'd lied. Wouldn't he? But if she actually believed that, why did she keep putting off telling him the truth? What had happened to all the bravery she'd felt a couple of days ago? She knew. A couple of days ago she had only liked him. Now she realized she was falling in love with him and didn't want to lose him. Maybe with time he would fall in love with her. Then he would understand and be more likely to forgive her.

"I'm not hurting any longer. I haven't been for a long time." She sat up and scooted closer to him. She didn't want him to have any doubts about what she wanted. "And maybe I can help you work things out. Just let me."

She brushed her lips against his, then moved back and smiled at him. She really did want to help him move forward.

They could move forward together.

Brandon pulled Arden toward him until she was sitting in his lap and placed his lips on hers. Even as their lips met he knew he was making a mistake by giving in to his desires. She wasn't the kind of woman who gave her body without her heart coming along for the ride. He knew her feelings for him were growing. That was bad enough. Worse was admitting to himself that his feelings for her were stronger now, too. Despite his attempts to keep her at a distance, he was constantly drawn closer in a way he'd never been with another woman.

And it scared him silly.

But still. The feel of her lips beneath his was too good to resist. She tasted like the chocolate icing he'd caught her licking off a cupcake earlier. The sight of her tongue sliding across the treat had been so arousing he'd known he had to get away from her before his desire overcame his common sense. He'd rounded up a group of kids for an impromptu game of water volleyball. The cold water had cooled his body but done nothing to the fire that was still raging inside at this moment. The inferno had been burning too long for him to even try to extinguish. He slanted his head and deepened the kiss.

The sound of someone loudly clearing her throat

forced them apart. "Well, well. Maybe I need to get a chaperone for the chaperones."

Brandon shook his head. "Joni, did anyone ever tell you your timing was rotten?"

"No one I ever listen to."

"Then I won't waste my breath."

Arden slid off his lap and he immediately missed her slight weight. In that moment he knew that he wanted her with him forever. Despite his best efforts not to, he'd fallen in love with her. She'd managed to work her way inside his heart. He loved her. More than that, he trusted her. The walls he'd built around his heart after the debacle with Sylvia had fallen and crumbled into dust. Even thinking of Sylvia was no longer painful. It was as if the entire relationship had happened in another life. Or to another person. The healing he'd heard about but didn't believe in had occurred. And the reason was clear. Arden.

Sweet Arden had healed his broken heart with her caring and innocent manner. He was ready to love again. To trust again. To open himself up to a relationship.

He needed some time to think about things and be absolutely sure of his feelings. He didn't want to act in haste and hurt Arden by accident. Or, worse, scare her off.

"I'll get to my post supervising the boys." Unable to stop himself, he reached out and caressed Arden's soft cheek. "Will you have dinner with me tomorrow night?"

She nodded and he left the room, happier and more optimistic than he'd been in years.

Chapter Thirteen

Arden removed the envelope from her door, then stepped inside her apartment. She pulled out the folded note.

I'll be by to pick you up at seven. Wear something casual and as beautiful as you are. Until tonight. B.

Her heart skipped a beat as she read the words again. A second later it plummeted to her toes. These weren't the words of a man who only wanted to be friends. Was Brandon interested in pursuing a relationship? Was she? Sure, her feelings for him had changed and grown as she'd gotten to know him better. But was she ready for something real? Now that it was looking like a distinct possibility she had a few doubts. Just how would a relationship work? They lived and worked in two different states.

No matter what else did or didn't happen, she had to tell him the truth. She couldn't expect to start a relationship with him as long as there was deception between them.

Oh, why had she let this go on for so long? Why had she lied in the first place? Okay, she remembered why. Still, she wished she had thought things through before giving Brandon a false name. Hadn't she always gotten into trouble by being impetuous?

Well, she couldn't change the past. And she might be jumping to conclusions. She could be reading more into this date than he intended. The only way to know for sure would be to let the night unfold. Then she would know for sure.

It couldn't hurt anything to look and smell her best. If she hurried, she would have enough time for a bubble bath. Flipping through her closet, she pulled out a pair of peach capris she'd bought at the boutique on an impromptu shopping trip. The pants were well made and fit her like a glove. Best of all, they matched a top she'd brought with her from Baltimore. She'd pair them with low-heeled sandals and knock Brandon's socks off.

Brandon inhaled and knocked on Arden's door. He held a bouquet of pink and cream roses in his right hand and a box of Louanne's chocolate-covered almonds in his left. He'd promised himself he would never put himself out there again where his heart could be trampled, and yet amazingly here he stood, ready to begin a relationship with a woman he'd known only a few weeks. A woman planning to leave town soon. Unless he found a way to convince her to stay. He must be crazy to take this kind of risk again, yet here he was.

The door swung open and she stood there looking as lovely as anyone he'd ever seen. For a moment he was struck dumb. Her eyes lit up when she saw him and his heart leaped in response.

"Hi." She sounded breathless and excited as she noticed the flowers and candy. "Are those for me?"

"Only you."

"Thank you. They're beautiful. And you know I love chocolate." She stepped aside. "Come on in."

The roses were already in a vase so all she needed to do was set them on the breakfast bar. She looked longingly at the candy before setting it beside the flowers. She turned to face him and suddenly seemed a bit shy. "I hope I'm dressed all right."

She looked delicious in her cropped peach pants and fitted print top. "You're dressed just fine."

"So where are we going?"

"It's a surprise."

"Will you give me a hint?"

"Nope."

"What if I guess?"

"Still no."

She giggled and grabbed her bag. "Well, then, let's get going. The sooner we get there, the sooner my suspense will end."

"In that case, maybe I'll take the scenic route."

"Do that and I'll sing that song you hate."

"Direct route coming right up."

"Is this my surprise?" Arden asked breathlessly. She had never seen anything so romantic.

Brandon nodded. "Yeah. I hope you like it."

A canopy had been erected on a secluded section of the beach. The starry sky provided the perfect backdrop. Inside there was a table draped with a pink cloth and two chairs. Candlelight flickered in a globe, softly illuminating the area. Glass vases filled with pink and yellow roses lined the path to the entrance. The wind blew the perfumed air, teasing Arden's senses. The sound of waves lapping against the shore filled the silent night. She sighed with pleasure. "It's beautiful. How did you do this?"

"A friend of mine owns one of the new beachfront homes. He's out of town for the night and let me use his place." Brandon led her to the table and pulled out a chair. Still overwhelmed by the absolute beauty and romance of it all, she sat.

He gestured to a person she hadn't noticed before as he took the seat across from her. A young man dressed in a black shirt and pants appeared seemingly out of nowhere carrying a bottle of wine, which he handed to Brandon. Arden recognized Tim as a waiter who worked at Heaven on Earth. She smiled at him.

Tim grinned, nodded and disappeared as quietly and quickly as he had arrived. Brandon expertly opened the bottle and filled their glasses. He raised his in a toast. "To a wonderful evening."

Arden smiled and sipped her wine. "This is delicious."

"It's from my private collection."

The young waiter returned carrying a tray of appetizers that he placed in front of them before once more vanishing.

"I heard you once say that you loved crab cakes so

I worked up a new recipe just for you." Brandon gestured toward her plate. "Try one and let me know what you think."

If the tantalizing aroma was any indication, they were going to be beyond delicious. She took a bite and flavor burst through her mouth. "Oh, this is great. Better than great. I could be happy eating crab cakes for the main course."

"You only say that because you don't know the rest of the menu. I've tried to create a meal that includes all of your favorites."

Arden's heart nearly exploded with happiness. He was definitely spoiling her. No one had ever put so much effort into making her happy.

As she ate course after magnificent course her joy grew so that she was nearly overwhelmed. By the end of the meal, as she dug into her chocolate brownie, the sound of violins filled the air.

"Boy, this dessert is better than I thought. I'm hearing music."

Brandon chuckled. "I can't take credit for that. I brought a CD of my favorite music and asked Tim to play it when he brought out dessert. I thought it would be a nice touch."

"It's perfect. This has been the most perfect night."

Brandon reached out and gently wiped a few crumbs from the corner of her bottom lip. His hand lingered and caressed her cheek. In his eyes she saw a flicker of desire that matched the longing growing inside her. "The night isn't over yet."

Her heart leaped, then stuttered before returning to beat at its normal pace. Brandon put his napkin on his empty dessert plate and she followed suit. He reached

out a hand and she took it, following him to the edge
of the water. Waves lapped against the shore, leaving
damp sand in their wake. They removed their shoes
and walked in the warm water. She smiled as she remembered the night they'd met. She'd waded in cold
water then and was chilled to the bone. Nothing about
her was chilled now. If anything she was overheated.

Brandon clasped Arden's hand, her small palm
pressed against his. Her hand felt even softer against
his calluses. Nothing had ever felt this right. He'd been
involved with women many times in his life, but he had
to admit he'd never experienced the connection with any
of them that he shared with Arden. Even the feelings
he'd had for Sylvia, someone he'd proposed to, paled
in comparison. Nothing in his past prepared him for
the depth of emotion Arden awakened in him. Those
emotions were growing rapidly and showed no signs of
slowing down or diminishing.

He'd been fighting his feelings from the beginning,
trying to convince himself he was infatuated and that
it would all blow over. His life would return to normal and Arden would fade into the background. His
restaurant would once more be the entire focus of his
life. Instead, she continued to occupy his thoughts. He
wanted to spend more time with her. Despite his inten-
tion to hold her at a distance, he repeatedly found himself drawn to her. Like any wise man, he knew when he
was beaten. So he stopped fighting. No longer worried
about defending his heart, he decided to try to win hers.

The old saying about food and a man's heart also
applied to women. As a chef he had that nailed. One
of the first things he'd noticed about Arden was her

love of food. Too many women came close to starving themselves in order to attain a Photoshop size that didn't exist in the real world. At least not among healthy adult females. Arden enjoyed eating and didn't care who knew. Nothing appealed to a chef more than someone who delighted in his food. So he'd prepared a lavish feast for her and she'd clearly enjoyed it.

Arden squeezed his hand, and he looked down and returned her smile. They walked in easy silence, the only sound the slap the steady waves made as they softly crashed against the sand before the foam caressed their bare feet. The moonlight shone brightly, spotlighting her delicate features. A gentle breeze blew against his skin and Arden's tempting scent filled the air.

An unusually strong wave crashed against their legs, causing Arden to stumble against him.

"Sorry," she murmured.

"What, getting knocked down by a rogue wave isn't on your bucket list?"

"Believe it or not, very few things on that list involve water." She scooped a handful of water and tossed him a mischievous look before letting the water drain through her fingers. Smiling, she splashed and scampered across the beach.

He followed more slowly, enjoying the sway of her hips in her tight pants. She found a place that appealed to her and sat down, stretching out her legs. He sat beside her on the sand. He could feel the warmth of her smaller body, heating him in a way the sun never could. She turned toward him, still laughing. There were a few grains of sand clinging to her cheek and, without thinking, he lifted his finger to her cheek and brushed them away. No matter how often he touched her skin, he was always amazed by just how soft it was. "Please tell me kissing on a moonlit beach made the cut and is on the list."

She leaned into his hand. "It is as of now."

He needed to feel her in his arms, to taste her lips and hear her whisper his name on a sigh. His body was hard with need, his passion held back by a single thread. Despite the intense longing surging through his body, Brandon slowly lowered his head until his lips barely brushed hers, keeping the pressure light.

He could do this. He could allow them some pleasure without crossing the line making return impossible. Although Arden wasn't as vulnerable as she had been when they'd met, her heart had still been battered. She shouldn't be rushed. He needed to be patient and give her time to fall in love with him.

She moved closer and increased the pressure with her own lips, opening to him. Her hands gripped his shirt, pulling him to her, and the thread snapped. His control gone, he wrapped her in his arms and kissed her with all the longing that had been building for weeks, allowing himself this brief moment of heaven.

Beneath the flavor of the chocolate dessert was a sweetness that Arden alone could claim. One sample simply wasn't enough. It was as if he'd been stranded on a deserted island, slowly starving, and now was being gifted with pure nectar of the gods.

Arden's sigh beneath his lips was nearly his undoing. He called upon a discipline he'd never had to use before and reluctantly ended the kiss. Breathing hard, he brushed a trembling finger against her kiss-swollen lower lip and leaned his forehead against hers.

"Wow," she breathed, her breath a sexy whisper against his face.

He exhaled. "Yeah, wow."

"So now what?"

Good question. "Now I take you home and we say good-night." Even though everything in him screamed in protest, he forced himself to stand, then reached a hand to her.

She was silent for a long moment. "Must we?"

The reluctance in her voice matched his. He didn't want to end the night. At least not this way. But he was determined to stick to the vow he'd made earlier and not take the chance of making their relationship awkward by pushing her to make love. His resolve was weakening when every breath he took was filled with her totally distracting scent. There was no way he could concentrate when her very sexy body was within arm's reach. "It's late. Tomorrow will be here before you know it. I have to go to the markets in the morning."

She took his hand and he pulled her to her feet. Her soft breasts pressed into his arm and he nearly groaned aloud. Sometimes being a gentleman sucked.

She dusted the sand from the seat of her pants. "Do you mind if I go with you again?"

"Sure. That would be great." Brandon wasn't ready to say he'd fallen in love with her, but he definitely liked the idea of the two of them being together. Perhaps for the rest of their lives.

Chapter Fourteen

Arden blinked as the alarm clock blared from across the dark room. She'd learned the hard way the consequences of having the clock close enough for her to hit the snooze button repeatedly. Covering her head with her pillow, she tried to block out the persistent noise, but couldn't. Finally she sighed and sat up, then rose and stumbled across the room to stop the irritating sound.

She'd barely slept at all, so she was sleepier than normal. Then she remembered last night with Brandon and the reason she'd set the alarm and all sleepiness fled, leaving behind a blur of emotions. She wrapped her arms around her middle as she relived Brandon staring deep into her eyes before he lowered his head ever so slowly to kiss her. And what a kiss. Even now her toes curled at the memory. The sensation of his lips was like nothing she'd ever felt before and something she couldn't wait to experience again.

Although Brandon had told her he wasn't looking for a relationship, she believed his feelings had changed. Even though he hadn't said a word, his actions spoke for him. He cared for her. He often reached for her hand as they walked, holding it tight as if he didn't want to let her get too far from him. When she helped at the restaurant, she felt his eyes searching her out as soon as he entered the dining room. And when their eyes met, he always nodded and smiled, his eyes communicating more eloquently than any words could.

True, none of these things meant that he was falling in love with her. Still, a girl could hope. Especially since she was head over heels in love with him and her love for him grew each day. She still wasn't sure how it had happened, but her broken heart had healed and was functioning quite nicely. Now she knew she'd never been in love with Michael-the-twerp. It was only her pride that had been hurt. She hated how easily he'd duped her, but none of that mattered now. The only thing that did was Brandon. She hoped that he loved her as much as she loved him. If he wasn't there yet, that was okay. She'd give him as much time as he needed. But would any feelings he had survive when she revealed her secret?

She bit her lip. She needed to tell him the truth. Today. She had already let so many opportunities to come clean slip through her hands, each one another nail in her coffin. She knew how much Brandon valued honesty. He deserved to know her real name and identity. And he deserved to know why she'd kept it a secret. Having been on the receiving end of deception, she knew how much it hurt to be betrayed. It was worse when the person doing the deceiving claimed to love you.

She should have come clean when he'd told her about Sylvia's deception. That would have been the perfect time. Before then she hadn't known her using a fake name would echo a painful incident in his past. After he'd told her about Sylvia, every day that passed only made her look as if she didn't intend to tell him the truth.

Her stomach churned and she muttered an unlady-like swear word. She didn't look forward to the conversation they were about to have.

If only she'd been honest in the beginning, she wouldn't be in this pickle. Then again, if he'd known her last name he might not have taken the time to get to know her. And she might have been suspicious of his kindness, believing he'd had an ulterior motive. It didn't matter now. The past was over and done. She had to deal with now. She was helping at Heaven on Earth tonight. She'd tell him the truth after the restaurant closed.

Arden forced a smile and smothered the urge to yell at the young customer to make up her mind and choose something. Generally, indecisive diners didn't bother her; she'd patiently try to help them choose a meal they would enjoy. Tonight she didn't have the inclination to do that. The conversation she needed to have with Brandon weighed heavily on her mind. Her head ached with fear and anticipation.

She remembered how furious he'd been with Sylvia. True, he'd been physically injured because of the other woman's lies. She'd be just as angry with any person who put her life in danger like that. She was certain Brandon would see the difference in what she had done and what Sylvia had done. Wouldn't he? Man, she hoped so.

"Have you made up your mind?" Arden asked.

The conflicted twentysomething had been sure she wanted seafood-stuffed crepes when she'd first ordered. She'd changed her selection as each of her three companions ordered, mirroring their choice. Now she was opening her menu again.

"I don't know."

"How about I give you a few more minutes to decide what you want?"

Her three friends groaned. Arden knew how they felt.

"What do you think I should get?" the woman asked Arden.

"Everything you've selected tastes wonderful. If I were you, though, I'd go with the crepes. That is what you initially wanted."

The young woman bit her lower lip. "Okay," she said in a rush.

Arden scribbled the order while the other three clapped.

"Hurry before she changes her mind," said the young man sitting next to the woman.

"You'd better hope I don't change my mind about you," she teased. She smiled at Arden and lifted her left hand. An enormous emerald that matched the woman's eyes perfectly glistened on her ring finger. "We got engaged last night."

"Congratulations." Arden smiled and felt a sudden longing for a ring of her own with all the love it represented. An image of Brandon offering her one on bended knee flashed in her mind. She quickly banished it.

As if she'd conjured him up, Brandon emerged from the kitchen to make his customary visit to the dining room, starting in the back and moving toward the front.

Dressed impeccably in a tailored gray suit that emphasized his broad shoulders, he shook hands with a gray-
haired gentleman, then chatted briefly with the woman
seated across from him. Whatever he said must have
been amusing because they all laughed.

The front door opened, letting in more patrons. Suddenly an unusual hush filled the dining room. Conversation quieted and then stopped abruptly. There wasn't
even the sound of silverware connecting with plates.
Then a slow buzz grew as people began to talk excit-
edly. Arden shivered and the hair on the back of her
neck stood up as a sense of dread filled her. She heard
his voice and her stomach plummeted to her toes.

Jax.

Slowly she turned and saw her brothers. Her mind
was filled with horror. What were they doing here?

Her eyes returned to Brandon. He had ended his
conversation with the older couple and was now weav-
ing his way to the front of the restaurant to discover
the source of the unusual mood that had settled on the
room. Any second he'd encounter her brothers and the
jig would be up.

No. Brandon couldn't find out this way. He'd never
believe she'd meant to tell him the truth if he found
out her identity from someone else. She had to get her
brothers out of there before they ruined everything.
Dropping her pad, she brushed past two young women
who were being seated, mumbling an apology. Several
heads turned, including Brandon's, as she began a mad
dash to the front of the restaurant. It was as if she was
running through sludge. No matter how fast she pumped
her legs, she didn't seem to move.

She heard Margo, the hostess, asking if they had

reservations, followed by her brother's response in the negative. A tall man on crutches blocked her path and she could only watch as her world began to crumble around her.

"There are no openings for tonight, Mr. Wexford," Margo said apologetically. Neither of her brothers shunned the spotlight the way Arden did, so they were frequently the subject of celebrity gossip that passed as entertainment. There was no chance celebrity follower Margo wouldn't recognize them. Margo smiled her brightest and Arden knew she'd been correct. "Maybe I can check with the chef if you want to wait, Mr. Wexford. He is also the owner."

Before either of her brothers could respond, she signaled to Brandon, who joined them.

"These are Blake and Jackson Wexford," Margo said, giving special emphasis to the last name. "You know, of Wexford Industries. The hotel people. They don't have reservations, but I was hoping you could work out something for them."

"Thank you for the offer, but we aren't here to eat," Jax said. "We're here to see our sister. We were told she works here."

"Nobody with that last name works here," Brandon said. "You must have been misinformed."

Arden's heart pounded in her chest, her dread growing as she watched the events unfold. She'd waited too long to tell the truth. The man in her path finally made it to his seat and she was able to cross the remaining distance to the hostess station.

"No, we weren't. I'm looking right at her."

"Who?" Brandon's voice sounded puzzled and his head swiveled to encompass the dining room.

"Arden. Arden Wexford."

"Arden *Wexford*?" Brandon's quiet voice ripped through her as if her name had been shouted. He turned to her, confusion in his eyes, quickly followed by accusation and hurt. Then he blinked and the only expression that remained was red-hot fury. He swung an arm toward Blake and Jax. "Your brothers?" he asked, as if he needed to hear her confirm Jax's words.

A lump the size of a mountain appeared in her throat and all she could do was nod.

"I see." He turned his back to her and faced her brothers. "I guess I was wrong about her."

She flinched. He'd spoken to Blake and Jax, but the words were directed to her. But he hadn't been wrong to trust her. He wasn't wrong about the type of person she was. And he certainly wasn't wrong about her feelings for him. She was the one who had been wrong. She'd been wrong to continue to hide her identity from him once she'd discovered what a good man he was. She'd been wrong to not tell him of her growing feelings for him.

He started to walk away and she grabbed his arm. If he left this way he might never listen. And she had to tell him the truth. "Please let me explain."

He stiffened, then shook off her hand as if he found her touch distasteful. "Now you want to explain. You had your chance. Many chances. And to think…" He clenched his jaw and looked back at her brothers. "We don't have any open tables so you'll have to leave. And Arden, you can clock out. That way you can go with them."

"Brandon, please." She was begging, but she didn't care. Her pride would mean nothing if she didn't have Brandon.

"Actually, we'd like to talk to you, too," Blake said.

"Me?" Brandon narrowed his eyes.

"Why?" Arden asked suspiciously. How did they even know about Brandon? For that matter, how did they know she'd been working here? She hadn't mentioned it. They must have hired a private investigator to keep tabs on her. Apparently, they were only pretending to believe she could run her own life. And given the mistake she had just made with Brandon, they might be right.

But that was different. She hadn't become involved with the wrong man again. Her mistake had been taking too long to realize he was just as good as he seemed.

"I don't have time for this. I have a restaurant to run." Brandon turned on his heel and strode to the kitchen and away from her.

Jax took a step after him, but Arden stopped him with a hand on his arm. "He's working. We need to leave."

She looked around the dining room. People were beginning to eat and to pick up the strands of their conversation. She caught the eyes of several of the other waitstaff. Their expressions ranged from curious to confused to downright angry. Nobody liked being deceived and made to feel like a fool. No doubt about it. She'd lost more than her anonymity tonight. She'd lost friends.

Worse, she'd lost Brandon.

She lifted her chin and walked out of the restaurant with as much dignity as she could muster. When she felt the cool night air, she rounded on her brothers, her sadness morphing into fury. "What are you doing here?"

"Trying to keep you from making another stupid mistake," Jax replied.

Arden gasped and drew her hands to her chest as if to protect her heart.

"He didn't mean it the way it sounded," Blake interjected with a sharp look at Jax.

"Oh, I think he did. You two don't respect me. You never have. You treat me like a child. I've grown up but you refuse to see that." Her voice was a croak, as the hurt she'd tried for years to hide was revealed.

"If you're so grown-up, then why are you playing make-believe?" Jax demanded. "Adults don't pretend to be someone that they aren't. Or are you going to tell me that Danielson forgot your name?"

"You don't understand. And it isn't any of your business!"

"You're right. I don't understand. Don't tell me you're in that waitress getup because of your low salary as a teacher. You do get regular payments from your trust fund."

"He needed help."

"And you just volunteered. Next he's going to need money. Are you going to volunteer that, too? Blake already told me you plan on giving money to his sister."

"Jax. That's enough." Blake stepped in between Arden and Jax. "Come on, Arden. It's time to leave."

"I'm not getting into a car with him." She glared at Jax, wishing she had the power to vaporize him. Or that she could at least knock that smug look off his face. "I'll walk."

"You don't need to walk. I'll leave Jax here and drop you off. A little fresh air will do him some good."

"Fine." Arden let Blake lead her to a late-model luxury sedan and snatched open the door before he could. She stared straight ahead, her feelings a jumbled mess. She was angry and disappointed. And hurt. She wouldn't let herself feel the pain of losing Brandon now or she would cry. Instead, she let out her sense of betrayal. "I trusted you, Blake."

"I didn't do anything wrong. You wanted money for this community center. I don't usually make site visits, but I figured I could check it out and see you at the same time. I didn't know you were pretending to be someone else." He gave her a pointed look.

Arden huffed out a breath. As much as she wanted to blame her brothers for this mess, she knew the fault was hers. She was the one who'd lied over and over. When her friendship with Brandon had developed into a more romantic relationship, she should have come clean. She'd had plenty of opportunities and, like a coward, had let them pass by.

Heck, she should have been honest before then. She'd known almost from the time they'd met that Brandon was nothing like Michael-the-pit-stain. Brandon was as honorable a man as they came. He was a real live hero.

And because she hadn't given him enough credit— hadn't given him the trust he had earned—she'd lost him.

She couldn't imagine what he must be thinking. That was a lie. She knew exactly the painful thoughts that were circling his mind. He thought she was just like Sylvia, a woman who had lied to him about her identity. True, Arden had lied, too. But she hadn't played with his heart with no care as to whether or not she broke it. She cared very much. But nothing in her actions would tell him that.

If only he knew how much she loved him. If only he'd give her a second chance. This time she'd take the utmost care with his heart.

* * *

Brandon held his anger and hurt in check as he prepared meal after perfect meal. Ordinarily cooking soothed him in a way nothing else could. Tonight it didn't. He was more unsettled than he had ever been and had to rely on his training. It took all of his focus just to keep the orders straight.

The urge to smash something—anything—nearly consumed him, but he resisted the impulse. His grandfather would never have tolerated such behavior in anyone, much less his own grandson, and Brandon respected his memory too much to act that way. Besides, his employees were present and he wouldn't create a scene in their presence. They were already sneaking glances at him and murmuring about Arden. Apparently, news of her true identity had already made the rounds.

He stole a glance at the clock. What was taking the night so long to pass? The one time he needed to lose himself in the work, he couldn't. His usual pleasure in the kitchen was missing and all he wanted to do was leave. He needed to be alone where he could yell out his pain.

His mind kept replaying the scene in the dining room. He could see Arden's shocked and guilty face as she was caught in her lie. Would she ever have told him the truth? He doubted it. To her, the entire thing had been a lark. She'd been a bored heiress wanting to see how the other half lived. Fool that he was, he'd fallen for her act, believing every word she'd uttered while she'd laughed at him. He'd been falling in love while she'd been playing a game.

Frowning, he checked the finished meals on a tray and then nodded to the waitress. She touched his arm before she took it, and he saw the sympathy in her eyes.

Great. He'd become an object of pity among his employees. A moment later Joni rushed into the kitchen. Good news sure traveled fast.

"If you came to check on me, you shouldn't have bothered. I'm fine."

Joni glanced around the kitchen before speaking. Everyone was busy working, but she stepped closer and kept her voice down anyway. "You don't have to pretend with me. I know you're hurt by Arden's betrayal. I'm pretty furious with her myself."

He exhaled slowly. "She lied."

"I know."

He gritted his teeth at what a fool he'd been. Again. "You might believe every woman is not a liar, but you can't prove it by me. I should have kept my distance."

"At least give her a chance to explain."

"I don't need to hear an explanation or some lame excuse. All I want is for her to leave and never come back."

"Brandon."

"I can't take any more hits. Every time I open myself up, I end up on the losing end. I'm done, Joni. I'm done." He turned back to the stove, determined to put Arden out of his heart and mind.

Arden was sitting on the bottom step of her apartment when Brandon's truck swung into the driveway, headlights illuminating the rows of flowers lining the yard. Nerves set butterflies free in her stomach, and she circled her arms around her waist in a futile attempt to still the churning inside. Her body went suddenly weak and she wondered if her legs would hold her.

Brandon parked beside her car and slammed the

door. She heard him swear as he stalked angrily across the lawn. He stopped abruptly when he saw her. Nibbling on her bottom lip, Arden stood shakily and wiped her suddenly moist hands on her skirt.

"What are you doing here?" he asked.

"I wanted to talk."

"I'm not interested in what you want." He headed for his house, cutting through the grass. She ran to catch up, grabbing his arm. The look he shot her chilled her very soul. She had expected anger and disappointment, but this was something more. This was rage. Controlled rage, but rage, nonetheless. For the first time that night, she worried that he might not give her a chance to explain. And if he didn't understand, he'd never forgive her.

"Please, Brandon, just listen to me. Then if you still want me to go, I'll leave and stay out of your life. I promise." She'd already piled her belongings into the back of the Beetle and booked a room at the Come On Inn just in case.

He pulled away from her grasp and folded his arms across his chest. Those arms had once wrapped around her, providing protection and comfort. Now they created an impenetrable barrier between her heart and his. "You seem to believe you have a say in this. You don't. This is my home. My property. I let you stay in my apartment because I believed you needed a place to live. But you don't. So you can get out of my apartment and out of my life."

"I can explain everything if you would just listen."

"I don't want to hear your explanation. There is nothing you can say that will justify lying to me. If you wouldn't even tell me your real name, what else are you hiding?"

He climbed the back stairs to his house and she ran

to keep up with him. This was her one and only opportunity to talk to him. If he made it inside, the chance would be lost. "I love you," she yelled.

He stopped and spun around. "What?"

She exhaled and said more softly. "I love you."

"Don't even try it," he snarled. "You don't love me. You don't know what love is."

His words cut her to the bone and she staggered back from the impact. "It may look like that to you, but you're wrong. I love you with everything inside me."

"You've got a funny way of showing it. I may not be an expert on the methods of expressing love, but I know lies and deceit aren't among them. You might want to remember that the next time you decide you *love* someone. He might not appreciate being involved with a liar any more than I do."

Arden sucked in a painful breath. When she spoke her voice trembled with emotion. "There won't be anyone else. I won't love anyone else because my heart belongs to you."

"I don't want your heart, Arden. Feel free to give it to another sucker. Then you can play all the games you want with his heart."

"It wasn't a game, Brandon. I just wanted you to like me for me."

He climbed the stairs and disappeared into his house. A moment later the door closed firmly and the lock clicked into place. She sank to the ground and cried. It was over.

Standing inside the kitchen, Brandon steeled his heart against the sound of Arden's heartrending sobs. No doubt she wanted him to hear, run to her like a fool and say all was forgiven. She probably was only crying crocodile tears. She was nothing if not a world-class actress. She'd certainly had him fooled. He'd believed she was as honest as they came. Instead, she was no different than Sylvia. In fact, she was worse.

At least Sylvia had a justifiable reason for her lie. She was trying to bring down the drug dealer who'd killed her brother. Arden had just been looking to amuse herself, pretending to be a regular person when she was from one of the wealthiest families in the country. How she must have laughed at him. No doubt she and her worthless friends would have a good chuckle at the expense of the country bumpkins she'd met in Sweet Briar. She could entertain for hours on end with details of their less-than-sophisticated ways.

He turned out the light and walked to his bedroom, refusing to turn his head when he passed the guest room. She hadn't stayed there in weeks, yet the scent of her perfume lingered in the air as if taunting him.

His mistake had been getting seriously involved with Arden. He'd foolishly opened his heart to her and basically let her move in. He thought he'd learned his lesson with Sylvia. Somehow he'd let Arden convince him to take a risk again. What an idiot. That was a mistake he was never going to make again. He let himself feel the pain, searing it into his memory so that he'd never forget this agony. No woman was ever getting close to his heart again. In the future he would limit his involvement with women to brief and unemotional encounters.

The old gullible Brandon Danielson was gone for good.

Chapter Fifteen

Brandon frowned at the first rays of sunlight streaming through his window. He'd barely slept, but he needed to get to the markets. His assistant manager, Marcus, had offered to go, but Brandon refused to allow Arden to control his actions. She may have made a fool of him with her lies, but he would not allow her to diminish him in the eyes of his employees. He'd recovered from a woman's treachery before and he could do it again. He would carry on as he always had.

Twenty minutes later he pulled into the parking lot at the fish market. He was nearing the store when he heard his name being called. He recognized the voice and spun around, fury and joy battling for dominance inside him.

Arden stepped away from her car and tentatively crossed the lot until she stood directly in front of him. Despite his anger at her, he couldn't help but notice how lovely she looked in white denim shorts that hit midthigh and a purple floral top that clung to her breasts. The wind ruffled her short curls and she lifted a delicate hand and pushed the locks out of her eyes. Although she clearly hadn't gotten any more sleep last night than he had, she still was more beautiful than any woman he'd ever seen. She nibbled her full bottom lip, something she always did when she was nervous.

Irritated with himself for remembering that habit of hers, he stepped around her without speaking and headed toward a small fish store.

"Brandon, wait. Please."

He heard the anguish in her voice but suppressed his concern for her. There was no way he was going to feel compassion for someone who didn't care a bit about him. He stopped but didn't turn around. "What are you doing here?"

She stepped around him until they were face-to-face. Her familiar scent teased his nostrils. "You wouldn't listen to me last night."

"So you took that to mean I'd listen to you today?"

"I hoped you had time to cool off." When he didn't respond she rushed on, her words running into each other. "I know you think the worst of me, but I wish you'd just listen. Please."

Brandon told himself to ignore the begging in her voice and the sorrow on her face. He might have succeeded in doing that, but he couldn't ignore the tears that glistened in her eyes no matter how badly he wanted to. "Fine. You've got five minutes."

He grabbed her elbow and led her to a secluded area away from the stores where they wouldn't be disturbed. Leaning against a light pole, he folded his arms against his chest so he wouldn't give in to the traitorous desire to touch her. He remembered all too well how soft she felt and longed to experience that sensation just one more time before she was out of his life forever. "Well, talk."

Arden seemed to shrink at his words and she looked at him with hurt in her eyes. "I was going to tell you my real name last night."

"Of course you were."

"I'm telling the truth."

He raised an eyebrow and steeled his heart. He'd been down this road before. Luckily, this time bullets weren't involved so there was no risk of being killed. Too bad the pain in his heart was just as bad if not worse.

She huffed out a breath and rubbed her hands against her shorts, another sign of just how nervous she was. "Let me start at the beginning."

He shrugged. "This is your show. Use your time however you want. But in five minutes, I'm gone."

"My name is Arden Isabella Wexford. I'm the youngest child of Winston and Lorelei Wexford. The Wexford name is well-known in Baltimore. Heck, it's well-known all over America. People treat me differently because of my family name."

"Poor little rich girl."

"You said *I* had five minutes to talk."

He waved a hand at her. "I'm just letting you know I don't understand why you decided it would be fun to use a fake name and create a whole new persona."

"It wasn't like that. At least not at first. I had been involved with someone who was only with me because he wanted to get his hands on my money. Can you maybe understand how much that hurt? I was through with guys like that. I was through with guys, period. That experience made me cautious. I didn't trust my judgment anymore."

"And you thought I would do the same? I don't want your money, Arden. I never did." It was amazing how deeply it hurt to realize how little she thought of him.

"I know that now. But at the time I didn't know anything about you. And I wasn't planning on staying in Sweet Briar any longer than it took to get my car fixed. But then everything changed. You needed a waitress. You'd helped me and I wanted the opportunity to return the favor.

"I started making friends and became a part of this wonderful close-knit community. I have never felt such a sense of belonging in all my life. It felt so good I just didn't want to give it up. Then I fell in love with you and knew I had to tell the truth. I just hadn't figured out how."

Although part of him wanted to believe her, he couldn't take that leap. His trust had been battered too badly to take her at her word. He knew how skillfully she lied. She'd had him believing every word she said and none of it had been true. He'd fallen for a deceitful woman twice now. That was two times too many. "Is that the whole story? Because if you're telling me you lied because you didn't want people to know you were rich, that doesn't change my mind about you."

Her head dipped and she didn't respond. Apparently, she had nothing more to say.

Disappointment flooded him. He'd hoped to hear an explanation that would somehow warrant forgiveness for her lies. Instead, she'd revealed how she'd questioned his character. He pushed away from the post. "Time's up. Have a nice life."

She jumped in front of him and grabbed his arm. "Remember I told you a relationship I was in ended badly? What I didn't tell you was that I caught my boyfriend and my supposed best friend hiding cameras around his bedroom. He was planning on making a secret sex tape. Once he had the tape he planned to blackmail me. He was going to post it on the internet if I didn't give him a million dollars. He didn't care about me. He only wanted my money."

Brandon sucked in a breath. He'd run into some low-lifes in his time, but this guy took the cake. He could only imagine how deeply Arden had been hurt. Yet, that didn't give her the right to turn around and play games with him. *He* hadn't been after her money. "That's low. And I hope he gets what is coming to him. But that didn't give you the right to deceive me."

She sagged as if all the fight had gone out of her. "I just want you to understand where my head was when I arrived. I had planned to seclude myself in my parents' Florida home so I could lick my wounds in private. But then I met you and Joni. I liked you both so much. You became my friends."

"Why lie?"

She shrugged. "I liked being a regular person. You called me a poor little rich girl, and to you my problems might seem petty. But you have no idea what it feels like to never be sure who your friends are. People have tried to use me all of my life. It felt good to know you liked me for who I am and not what I have. Then we got closer and I knew I had to tell you the truth. So many times I opened my mouth to tell you."

"But you didn't." And that was the crux of the matter. Her voice dropped. "No. I didn't."

"I can understand keeping your identity a secret when you arrived. You didn't know anything about me. But once we were close, continuing to deceive me is beyond comprehension. And after I told you about Sylvia, continuing to deceive me is unforgivable."

"I know that now. But then…"

"So…what? This was a test? I had to prove myself worthy of knowing the truth? Worthy of being in a relationship with you?"

"That's not what I meant. I had been wrong before and didn't trust myself to be right about another man."

"Well, regardless of what you meant to do, that's what you did. I opened myself up to you. I shared my thoughts and feelings with you in a way I hadn't with anyone else before. And you were lying to me the entire time. I can't forgive that. Now, if there's nothing else, I need to get going before all the freshest seafood is gone. I still have a restaurant to run."

She shook her head, blinking rapidly. "Doesn't anything I say make a difference?"

"No." He turned around and left, forcing himself not to look back.

He had to consign Arden to a past he wouldn't revisit.

"What are you doing here?" Brandon sneered as he got out of his truck in the restaurant parking lot. The last people in the world he wanted to see were Arden's brothers. Wasn't dealing with one Wexford enough for today? He huffed out an impatient breath, then slammed his truck door.

"We want to talk." Blake Wexford was the elder and

had the reputation of being the more controlled of the two. And wasn't Brandon annoyed with himself for knowing that and anything else about the Wexfords? He'd berated himself most of the night for not recognizing Arden. It didn't matter that no one else had known who she was, either. Unable to sleep, he'd spent hours last night searching the internet for information about her. Impossible as it might seem, there wasn't a single picture of her anywhere. There was barely a mention of her name. That must have cost big bucks. When you were as wealthy as the Wexfords anything was possible, but there had been plenty of information about her brothers and he'd read it all.

"I've spoken to my quota of Wexfords for the day."

"You talked to Arden?" Jax, the more annoying one, butted in. Brandon hadn't needed to read an article about Jax to know that. He'd reached that conclusion at the restaurant last night. And since that question didn't warrant an answer, Brandon didn't give him one.

"We only want a minute of your time," Blake said.

"I'm working." He pushed past them and opened the tailgate of his truck. They followed.

Jax looked at the crates of fresh food with undisguised disdain and then back at him. "This won't take long. Then you can get back to whatever you were doing."

That pissed him off. Did this guy ever utter a word that wasn't condescending? Brandon might not be the CEO of a major corporation, but no one disrespected him. He closed the hatch and leaned against the bumper, arms crossed over his chest. "I'll tell you what. How about I barge into your office at Wexford Industries sometime when it's convenient for *me* and you stop whatever you're doing. Then we'll talk."

"You might have enough time on your hands to do that sooner than you think," Jax said.

Brandon pushed off the bumper and closed the distance between himself and the other man. He wasn't violent by nature, but he was angry enough to make an exception. "Just what are you saying?"

"I'm saying stay away from my sister or you'll wish you had."

He already wished he had, but there was no way he would admit it to this arrogant jerk. "Who I see or don't see is my business."

"And Arden is ours. She's always had guys trying to use her for her money. She doesn't need another one."

"I know it must be hard for you to believe, but I don't want Arden's money. I never did. Maybe if you actually took the time to get to know your sister, you'd see that she is enough of a prize on her own. She doesn't need money to get or hold on to a man."

The brothers exchanged a look Brandon couldn't decipher. "I've got to go. If you want more of my time, make an appointment."

Jax blocked his path. "You expect me to believe her trust fund doesn't matter. You would be the first."

"You don't have to believe it. I don't care. The truth is, I no longer want Arden." Brandon grabbed a crate of fruit and pushed past Arden's brothers.

But as Brandon walked away, he realized what he'd just said was as far away from the truth as he could get.

Chapter Sixteen

Arden pulled into the circular drive in front of her parents' Baltimore home. Her Beetle drove like new since John's repairs, but she couldn't drive it without thinking of Brandon and Sweet Briar, so she drove the Mercedes that usually sat in her garage.

The past week without Brandon had been so lonely. Even now her heart ached as she thought of the last time she'd seen him at the fish market. That morning she'd managed to keep her tears from falling until he was no longer in sight. How could something so wonderful have turned into heartbreak so fast?

Maybe they weren't meant to be. Given his past, it might not have mattered to Brandon when she told the truth. Once she'd given a false name, she had poisoned their relationship and made it easy for him to say goodbye. She should have known him well enough to understand that he wouldn't change his mind about her.

There had been no point in her staying in Sweet Briar, so she'd driven straight from the markets and out of town that very day, not stopping to say goodbye to anyone. The friends she'd made had been friends of Brandon and Joni, so they probably didn't care that she'd left.

Now that she was home she had to try to put the pieces of her life back together. She wasn't the same person who'd run away all those weeks ago. She never would be again.

She couldn't think about how she'd run away from Michael-the-hairball without feeling ashamed. What had she been thinking? He had been the one in the wrong. And she was not going to let him get away with it. There was no way he should be in a position of power over anyone, but especially not innocent children. She intended to let the school board know just what kind of person they had running one of their middle schools.

She hated to admit it, but her brothers had been right. Adults not only didn't play make-believe, they didn't pretend they were ostriches, burying their heads in the sand in the hope that their problems would vanish. It was time for her to act like the adult she was.

Her decision to report Michael to the school board would impact more than just her. It would affect her family, as well. The meeting before the board would be private, but because of the nature of her allegations, it might attract the attention of the local papers. It wouldn't make a ripple in the national press if her name really was Arden West. But as a Wexford, anything she did that was even slightly newsworthy would be a field day for the media. She'd always tried to live under the radar and go about her business like most people. She wouldn't be able to maintain her low public profile once this story broke. And that was okay. Some things were worth the sacrifice.

She turned off the car and quickly mounted the stone stairs leading to the family mansion. Despite the fact that the house had twenty rooms and was situated on seven acres, it had always felt homey to her. She gave her parents credit for that. They may have been wealthy, but she and her brothers had been raised with middle-class values. Winston and Lorelei had never been overly concerned with maintaining a certain type of public image. She had no doubt her parents would support her, but she did feel they deserved advance notice so they wouldn't be blindsided.

"Welcome home," her mother said, pulling her into a warm, perfumed embrace the moment Arden stepped inside.

"I should be saying that to you," Arden replied with a laugh. "You're the one who just got back from vacation last night."

"True. But I understand you had a bit of an adventure yourself."

"I take it you spoke to one of my brothers."

"Both. You know they can't hold water."

No. She was the one gifted with the ability to keep a secret. Now it seemed like a curse.

"Come on. Everyone is in the family room."

Arden walked beside her mother around the central staircase to the room where her family usually gathered. She heard the murmur of jovial conversation as she and her mother stepped inside the room.

"Well, little girl, are you going to just stand there, or are you going to give your old dad a hug?"

Arden pretended to ponder the question for a moment, then rushed into her father's arms. "I feel like it has been forever since I've seen you."

"The feeling is mutual." He tightened the embrace and held her for a moment longer. Arden inhaled the familiar scent of butterscotch candy. Winston Wexford had a sweet tooth he had passed down to her. She closed her eyes and recalled their many trips to the candy store after her Thursday-night dance lessons when she'd been in grade school. She hadn't enjoyed ballet a bit, but she had loved the secret candy runs they had made on the way home. Her three-year dancing career had lasted two years longer than it would have but for those trips.

"So, what's this I hear about you getting involved with a chef?"

Arden glanced at her brothers. Blake shrugged and Jax smirked. She was past caring. "I met a guy, but that's over. I need to talk to all of you about something else altogether."

"It sounds serious."

"It is." Arden looked around the room. Her family settled into comfortable chairs, then waited for her to start talking. "I don't know where to start."

"The beginning always worked for me," her father said. He turned an affectionate glance toward her mother. "But your mother always preferred to start with the most shocking part and then move backward. Whatever works best for you. We've got all day, right, boys?"

Blake and Jax nodded, but Arden knew they would prefer the CliffsNotes version, which was good because she didn't feel inclined to go into the dirty details.

"I'm going to the school board to try to get Michael Wallace removed from his position as principal at my school." She waited for the explosion of questions but none came.

Her father simply nodded once. "I'm sure you have your reasons."

"Yes." No one spoke and she knew they wouldn't. It was her story to tell at her pace. "He's a jerk but, more, he can't be trusted. Especially around kids. I'm telling you this because when the press finds out it might get ugly.

"I caught him hiding cameras in his bedroom so he could make a secret sex tape. With me. He thought he could blackmail me with it." She felt her cheeks warming and suddenly found a spot on the wall incredibly interesting and stared at it.

Jax leaped to his feet. "I'm going to kill him."

"I'm going to help," Blake added, hurrying behind his brother.

"Stop right there."

Blake and Jax froze at their father's quiet voice.

"Come back and sit down." He waited until they had returned to their chairs before continuing. "Since when do we use violence to solve our problems?"

"Since some jerk decided to hurt our sister," Jax replied angrily. "You can't mean to let him get away with this."

"No one is saying he is getting away with anything. Let's listen to Arden."

"All she wants to do is have him fired," Jax scoffed. "That's not enough."

"You're not the injured party, Jackson, so the decision isn't yours."

Jax breathed loudly through his nose, reminding Arden of a bull. It touched her to see her brothers so ready to defend her. Thankfully, she was strong enough to defend herself now. "I appreciate that you guys want to take care of me. I'm strong enough now to handle it myself."

"Is that the reason you ran away?"

Arden didn't shy away from Blake's words. She had run away rather than fight, so there was no reason to pretend she hadn't. She lifted her chin. "Yes. I didn't know what to do and I was too ashamed and embarrassed to come to any of you."

"Why?" His tone was a mixture of confusion and what sounded like hurt.

"I knew nobody liked Michael. I'd made a bad choice."

"You're not alone there," her father added. "We've all made mistakes."

"I know that now." She cleared her throat. "Anyway, I just want to take away Michael's power as much as I can. I have evidence I recorded on my phone of him telling someone his plans. It's all in the audio file. The school board can take it from there. If the police need a statement I'll give them one. What happens after that won't matter a bit to me. I am sorry if it makes the news, though." She looked at Jax, who was still seething, his breathing loud.

"Is that really all you want?" Jax demanded. Clearly he didn't agree with her decision, but he respected their father's authority and wouldn't go against him. And maybe her brother trusted that she knew what was best for her.

"It is."

"Fine. If that makes you happy."

"It will." Or at least as happy as she could be, given her broken heart.

"We're here if you need us," her mother said, and her father nodded. "And we're proud of you."

"Thank you."

After that, her father and brothers began to discuss business, and Arden and her mother left them to it. Lorelei wrapped her arm around Arden's shoulder. "Tell me more about the man you met."

"Oh, Mom. I messed up. I love him and I hurt him so badly."

"How?"

Arden explained about Brandon's past with his former fiancée. "And then I did the exact same thing she did."

"So what are you going to do now? I understand why you felt the need to come home to straighten out things with the school board, but how are you going to make things right with Brandon?"

If only she could. "He's done with me. He doesn't love me anymore. I'm going to respect his feelings and stay out of his life."

"If his love died that easily, it wasn't real."

"It was real, Mom," Arden replied instantly. She knew that for sure.

"Then fight for it. Love is too precious to let slip through your fingers."

"But what if he can't forgive me?"

"Then you'll know that you gave it all that you had. Don't run away just because you're afraid of getting hurt. The worst thing in the world would be to wake up next year and wonder what if. Do all that you can to set things right. Keep fighting for a second chance. If he loves you, it will work out in the end."

"You're right," Arden said, giving her mother a big hug. "You're absolutely right." And for the first time since she'd returned home, Arden could breathe without the constant pain in her heart. She wasn't happy, but if she could work things out with Brandon she would be. Somehow, some way, she was going to win him back. When the situation with the school board was settled, she was going to do some more running, this time toward something instead of away.

Chapter Seventeen

Brandon sampled the new shrimp appetizer he was creating, then dropped the fork on the counter with a loud clatter. Even though all the ingredients were mixed properly, the taste was off. In fact, nothing he had cooked the past two weeks tasted right. There was a bitter aftertaste that lingered even after the meal had been eaten. No one else noticed. People continued to rave over their food. The problem was with him. His heart wasn't in it. He'd never thought he'd see the day when he didn't enjoy cooking, but that day had arrived when he'd found out the truth about Arden. He couldn't believe he'd been such a fool again.

He'd always looked forward to Tuesdays so he could let his creative juices flow. That wasn't happening today. He dumped the food into a plastic container and snapped the lid closed. There was enough for Joni to take for lunch and share with her friends.

"I thought I'd find you in here."

He groaned. He loved his sister, but he couldn't handle another dose of her sympathy or her subtle defense of Arden. Joni really liked Arden and had been willing to give her friend the benefit of the doubt. Joni hadn't done anything overt to get him to change his mind, but she had let him know when Arden sent an enormous personal check for the youth center. Despite himself, he recalled how much fun he'd had with Arden volunteering at the center. The kids had really loved her enthusiasm. They had loved *her*.

He wiped a sponge across the counter and tossed it into the sink. "Actually, I'm on my way out."

"Why are you running away from me?"

That question froze him. "I'm not. I have to get to the restaurant."

"Sure."

He pulled his sister into a quick hug. "I'm fine, Joni. You don't need to worry about me."

"I hate that you're angry at me."

He reeled back in surprise. "Angry at you? Why would I be angry at you?"

"I encouraged you to date Arden and did everything I could to throw the two of you together. I even left town so you'd have some time alone. I'm sorry. I just thought she was a good person who could make you happy again. I was wrong and you got hurt. If I'd minded my own business you never would have gotten involved with her."

"None of this is your fault. I was attracted to Arden from the beginning. I spent time with her because I wanted to. And I'm not angry at you. Okay? Now I do need to get going. I have a bunch of paperwork waiting for me." He dropped a kiss on his sister's forehead, then headed out the door.

The restaurant was quiet when he arrived and headed to his office. The walls were a bright white, and framed photos of the restaurant in various stages of construction were hung in such a way that he could see them from his desk. They normally filled him with a sense of pride at what he'd accomplished. Today he felt nothing.

He raised the window to allow in fresh air, as well as sunlight. He'd wasted enough time stumbling around in the dark having his own personal pity party. His kind-hearted sister blamed herself for his poor judgment. That was unacceptable.

He rubbed his hand across his chest. Arden was out of his life. She'd gotten that message. Now he had to find a way to get her out of his mind. And then maybe he'd figure out a way to get her out of his heart.

He turned on his computer and opened the shift schedule. Before he could make changes based upon the number of advance reservations, his desk phone rang, its shrill sound shattering the silence. He idly checked the caller ID. What did Joni want now? Surely she wasn't checking on him again. Enough was enough. He let the call go to voice mail. A few seconds later there was a knock on his open office door. Looking up, he saw Marcus standing there. "What's up?"

"Sorry to disturb you, but Joni called and said to check your email. She sent you something she wants you to see right now."

"I'll get to it later." Brandon said, continuing to work.

Marcus stood there. Clearly Joni had told him not to leave until Brandon had done what she asked.

"Fine," Brandon huffed, then pulled up his email, opening the one from Joni. She hadn't written anything but had sent a link to an article. Curious, he clicked on it. It was a short video. He waited until it started. It was Arden. She was descending stairs of what looked like a government building surrounded by her family, a woman dressed in a suit by her side. Reporters called out questions to her and the cameras tightened to a close-up. She nibbled her bottom lip.

Despite the fact that he was still angry with her for not being honest, his heart clenched at the sight of her discomfort. A part of him he couldn't ignore wished he was there to stand between her and anything that hurt her.

His eyes hungered for her. It had been so long. She was as beautiful as he remembered, if slightly thinner. Her hair curled softly around her face and her eyes seemed to reach out and stare directly at him. In a moment, she got into a black sedan and sped out of sight.

The camera then turned to a reporter holding a microphone. "And there you have it. Arden Wexford, daughter of Winston Wexford, owner of Wexford Industries, leaving a meeting of the Baltimore school board where she testified against her former principal."

The reporter droned on for a minute, repeating information Arden had already shared with Brandon. He knew how hard having this information go public had to be for Arden. She guarded her privacy fiercely. And she had just put the most embarrassing moment in her life out there for people to discuss and decide if she was telling the truth. All because she believed secrets were dangerous. She hadn't known that before coming to Sweet Briar, so obviously she had grown. Good for her.

But what did that have to do with him? Did he care? Did she even care about him anymore?

Suddenly filled with energy, Brandon headed for the kitchen. He did some of his best thinking while cooking. And he had a lot of thinking to do. For the first time since Arden had left, he believed he could do some of his best creating.

One cutting-edge recipe for salmon later, Brandon had thought enough to realize he'd been wrong. Arden wasn't a self-centered rich girl looking for fun at his expense. She was a kind, loving woman who'd done what she thought best to protect herself. He was willing to admit that his past with Sylvia had affected the way he viewed all women, including Arden. If he felt justified in doing that, then surely she was justified in looking at men through the same lens as she'd seen her ex-boyfriend. Certainly she wouldn't be wrong in putting the lessons she'd learned in the past to use.

He was able to admit that one of the lessons she'd learned was that some people would sink to the lowest levels if they thought they could profit from it. Most people were honest, but there were enough greedy ones out there to make a wealthy woman wary. She'd be foolish not to be cognizant of that and to act accordingly. He didn't trust anyone blindly, so why should he expect her to? Arden was a product of her past, the same as he was.

As hard as it was to admit, her decision to use a fake name didn't have anything to do with him. She hadn't even known him, so it was a bit ridiculous to expect her to know his character.

Maybe it was time for them both to break away from their pasts and take a leap of faith. His parents might have the right idea, after all. Although he wasn't interested in dating any of the women they shoved in his path, they were right to urge him to get on with his life. It was time. Now he had to convince Arden to give him another chance.

Brandon stifled the urge to barge into Blake Wexford's office, waiting instead for the secretary to announce him. Once he'd reached the conclusion that Arden hadn't committed an unforgivable act, he'd wanted to get to her as soon as possible so they could start over. He first spoke to Joni, who'd been relieved that he was willing to give love a chance. She'd confessed that she missed her new friend horribly and urged him to do whatever was necessary to win Arden's heart again.

After assuring himself that Marcus could handle the restaurant for a couple of days, Brandon had tossed a change of clothes in a bag and hopped on the first plane to Baltimore. On the flight he'd prepared what he hoped was a speech that would convince Arden to forgive him and give them another shot. He hadn't quite worked out the details of how a relationship between them would work, given the fact that they lived in two different cities. He just knew that if she was willing, he would try.

"Mr. Wexford will see you now."

Rising, Brandon followed the woman through the quiet hallway to an open door. She stepped aside and gestured for him to enter. He thanked her and went in. He was surprised to see Arden's other brother, as well as her father. Obviously, this was going to be a family meeting. Good. That would save him some time. If they thought to intimidate him by their greater number, they were sadly mistaken.

"Thanks for seeing me," he said, extending his hand.

"My curiosity got the best of me," Blake said as he shook Brandon's hand. "You remember my brother, Jax. And this is our father, Winston Wexford."

Brandon shook each of the other men's hands. Blake offered drinks, but they all refused.

"So, what brings you to our fair city?" Winston asked once they were all seated.

"I'm here about Arden."

"Really? The last I heard you didn't want anything more to do with her," Jax said. "You not only let us know that loud and clear, you were blunt about that to her, too."

Brandon remembered the unshed tears glistening in Arden's eyes the last time he saw her, and his stomach knotted. "I regret the way I talked to Arden. That's not one of my proudest moments."

"Blake. Jax. Give us some privacy, would you?" Winston said.

"You're kicking me out of my office?" Blake asked in apparent disbelief.

Winston smiled. "Think of it as a chance for you to take a break."

Blake sighed and followed his brother out of the office. Brandon watched them go, wondering just what the elder Wexford was about to say that he didn't want his sons there.

"What do you mean you're here about Arden?"

Brandon rubbed a hand over his chin. Winston didn't strike him as the kind of man who would appreciate someone beating around the bush, so he decided to cut to the chase. "I hurt her badly. I want to set things right."

"What do you mean by right?"

"I love her. Setting things right would involve making sure she knows that."

Mr. Wexford's eyebrows shot up and he nodded. "Is that so?"

"Yes." Was that a hint of a smile on the older man's face? "You don't know me, but I'm prepared to tell you anything you need to know."

"I already know everything I need to about you. Arden and I had many talks. And then there are my sons. They've told me plenty. But to be honest, you showing up here tells me more about your character than anything else."

"So that's it?"

"I trust my instincts. They haven't led me astray very often. And my sons are very protective of their sister. They wouldn't have left this room if they thought you were up to no good."

"That other guy fooled them." And he had hurt Arden in the process.

"No, he didn't."

Brandon couldn't believe it was this easy. He'd come prepared to do battle for the right to be with Arden. "So you aren't going to threaten me with a fate worse than death?"

"Is there one?"

"Yes." He looked directly into Mr. Wexford's eyes. "Living without Arden."

That answer seemed to satisfy Arden's father.

"So what's your plan?"

"I'm still working on the details, but I know it will involve begging."

Winston laughed. "Throw in some chocolate and you just might have a chance."

Arden rode the elevator to the top floor that housed her father's office, silently rehearsing her speech. Packing had taken longer than she'd anticipated, so it was already nearly three. She wouldn't be able to leave until tomorrow, but since she wanted to start out early, she'd say her goodbyes now.

The conversation with her mother had gone better than she'd expected. Then again, Lorelei was a romantic at heart. Not that she wouldn't have let Arden know if she disagreed with her decision to return to Sweet Briar. Lorelei had seen how unhappy Arden had been with the way things ended with Brandon.

She could still hear her mother's words. *Give it everything you have. If it doesn't work, then at least you'll know you tried. Only then will you be able to go forward, even if your heart hurts for a while.* She just hoped her father agreed.

When she stepped from the elevator, she saw Jax and Blake huddled together in a corner. Odd, considering they each had their own office.

"What are you guys doing?"

"What does it look like?" Jax asked.

"Like you're loitering in the hall, waiting to pounce on some unsuspecting passerby."

Blake muttered something that sounded like, "Close." Was he pouting?

"What are you doing here?" Jax countered.

"Actually, I'm here to see you guys and Dad. Can we go to his office?"

"We can, but he's not there." Blake folded his arms over his chest.

"How do you know?"

"Because he just kicked me out of mine."

Goodness. He was pouting. Arden barely kept herself from laughing. The men in her family tended to be territorial about the craziest things. "Okay. Then let's go there."

"Why? What's so important?"

Arden sighed. She could practice on her brothers. "I'm going back to Sweet Briar."

"Why?" Jax straightened.

"The short answer is because that's where Brandon is."

"What's the longer answer?"

"I ran. I should have stayed and fought for us, but I didn't."

"So, you're going to just go back there unannounced?" Jax asked, his eyes narrowed.

"Yes. And I'm going to make him listen no matter how long it takes."

Blake looked over her shoulder. "I have a feeling it's not going to take all that long."

Arden turned and gasped. "Brandon." Her voice was reduced to a whisper. "What are you doing here?"

"I've come for you."

Her heart leaped at his words, yet she couldn't give it free rein. Not yet. "For me? But I thought… I thought you didn't want me."

He stepped closer and held out his hand. She automatically took it and let him lead her to the reception area and away from her family's eyes. "I want you,

Arden. You have no idea how much. I just needed to work through my own issues. I accused you of not trusting me, when I didn't trust you as much as I proclaimed. I'm sorry for that. I hope you can forgive me."

"I didn't know about your past when we met. But I am sorry for not telling you my real name sooner."

"A rose by any other name would smell as sweet. I believe Arden Wexford is just as perfect as Arden West."

"I'm not perfect. I'll make mistakes."

"So will I. But if we forgive as easily as we want forgiveness, everything will be okay."

Arden nodded. "I can."

"You obviously came here to see your family. I can wait while you talk to them."

"I was only going to tell them goodbye. I was on my way to Sweet Briar in the morning to convince you to give us another chance."

He smiled and it was as if a weight had been lifted from her shoulders. "How long were you planning on staying?"

"As long as it took to make you love me."

Brandon leaned in closer, his fingers gently cupping her face, his thumb teasing her lower lip, making her want to fall into his arms. "What's your plan?"

"I didn't think that far." Her voice was a mere whisper.

"Good thing I did. We can go with my plan."

"Which is?"

"First I make sure you know I love you. Then I convince you to stay forever."

Forever. It had a certain ring to it. "Sounds like a perfect plan to me."

His lips curved into a sexy smile before they covered hers. Forever might not be long enough, but it was a perfect start.

* * * * *

If you loved this story,
don't miss the first book in the
SWEET BRIAR SWEETHEARTS,
by Kathy Douglass

HOW TO STEAL THE LAWMAN'S HEART

Available from Harlequin Special Edition.

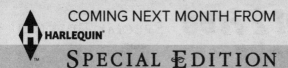

Get 2 Free Books,

Plus 2 Free Gifts—

just for trying the Reader Service!

"Munchy!" Cami cried. The mutt raced to greet her and
she dipped low to meet him.

Garrett waited, giving her all the time she wanted to pet
and praise his dog. When she finally looked at him again,
he explained, "The bear must have whacked him a good
one. When I found him, he was knocked out, but I think
he's fine now."

She submitted to more doggy kisses. "Oh, you sweet
boy. I'm so glad you're all right…"

When she finally stood up again, he handed over the
diamond ring and that giant purse.

"Thank you, Garrett," she said very softly, slipping the
ring into the pocket of the jeans she'd borrowed from him.
"I seem to be saying that a lot lately, but I really do mean
it every time."

"Did you want those high-heeled shoes with the red
soles? I can go back and get them…" When she just shook
her head, he asked, "You sure?" He eyed her bare feet.
"Looks like you might need them."

"I still have your flip-flops. They're up by the Jeep. I kicked them off when I ran after Munch." For a long, sweet moment, they just grinned at each other. Then she said kind of breathlessly, "It all could have gone so terribly wrong."

"But it didn't."

She caught her lower lip between her pretty white teeth. "I was so scared."

"Hey." He brushed a hand along her arm, just to reassure her. "You're okay. And Munch is fine."

She drew in a shaky breath and then, well, somehow it just happened. She dropped the purse. When she reached out, so did he.

He pulled her into his arms and breathed in the scent of her skin, so fresh and sweet with a hint of his own soap and shampoo. He heard the wind through the trees, a bird calling far off—and Munch at their feet, happily panting.

It was a fine moment and he savored the hell out of it.

"Garrett," she whispered, like his name was her secret. And she tucked her blond head under his chin. She felt so good, so soft in all the right places. He wrapped her tighter in his arms and almost wished he would never have to let her go.

Which was crazy. He'd just met her last night, hardly knew her at all. And yesterday she'd almost married some other guy.

Don't miss
GARRETT BRAVO'S RUNAWAY BRIDE
by Christine Rimmer, available October 2017 wherever
Harlequin® Special Edition books and ebooks are sold.

www.Harlequin.com

LOVE
Harlequin
romance?

Join our Harlequin community to share your thoughts and connect with other romance readers!

Be the first to find out about promotions, news, and exclusive content!

Sign up for the Harlequin e-newsletter and download a free book from any series at

www.TryHarlequin.com

CONNECT WITH US AT:

Harlequin.com/Community

 Facebook.com/HarlequinBooks

 Twitter.com/HarlequinBooks

 Instagram.com/HarlequinBooks

 Pinterest.com/HarlequinBooks

ReaderService.com

**ROMANCE WHEN
YOU NEED IT**

THE WORLD IS BETTER WITH

Romance

Harlequin has everything from contemporary, passionate and heartwarming to suspenseful and inspirational stories.

Whatever your mood, we have a romance just for you!

Connect with us to find your next great read, special offers and more.

f /HarlequinBooks

🐦 @HarlequinBooks

www.HarlequinBlog.com

www.Harlequin.com/Newsletters

HARLEQUIN®

A *Romance* FOR EVERY MOOD™

www.Harlequin.com